High Country Woman

"I want you to introduce me to your brothers," Cole said. "Otherwise, I might have a tough time, seeing as how I shot their sister."

"It's only a flesh wound," Nancy said. "It's already stopped bleeding, though the lining of this jacket's probably ruined."

"Get your mount," he said.

She nodded and started back through the timber for her horse. Cole admired the way she filled out her Levi's. Come bedtime, it looked like she'd have to peel them off. Maybe he was the man to help . . .

RED SKIES OVER WYOMING

Will C. Knott

Charter Westerns by Will C. Knott

RED SKIES OVER WYOMING
THE RETURN OF ZACH STUART
THE GOLDEN MOUNTAIN
LYNCHER'S MOON

WILL C. KNOTT

RED SKIES OVER WYOMING

CHARTER BOOKS, NEW YORK

RED SKIES OVER WYOMING

A Charter Book / published by arrangement with
the author

PRINTING HISTORY
Berkley edition / June 1980
Charter edition / May 1984
Second printing / September 1986

For information address: The Berkley Publishing Group,
200 Madison Avenue, New York, New York 10016.

ISBN: 0-441-71147-2

Charter Books are published by The Berkley Publishing Group,
200 Madison Avenue, New York, New York 10016.
PRINTED IN THE UNITED STATES OF AMERICA

One

COLE RANDALL reined in to let his father catch up. Mike Gunnison pulled up also and looked back at Cole and his father. Cole saw the troubled look on Mike's face and understood.

"This won't take a minute, Mike!" Cole called to the ramrod. "I'll tell Dad we don't need him."

"You think he'll listen?"

"All I can do is try."

Mike's narrow shoulders lifted in a shrug. He dropped his reins around his saddle horn and thumbed his hat back off his forehead, eyes alert, the trace of a smile on his lean, good-humored face.

Cole looked back at his rapidly approaching father. The man was galloping through the bluestem toward Cole, a grim cast to his granitelike face. He had dressed especially for

1

this confrontation, Cole realized. His father was wearing his best black suit, his tall gray Stetson, and a string tie that set off nicely the broadcloth shirt Consuelo had made for him only last week. As Cole pulled his horse around, the unpleasant thought occurred to him that his father might be thinking in terms of either a celebration or a funeral.

"Hold up, pa!" Cole said, riding up alongside his father. "Mike and I can handle this."

"I know you can, Cole. I just want to go along to put in my two cents—and tell that fool marshal what I think of him."

Cole shook his head in sudden vexation. "Let me handle this without your two cents, pa. It's time you gave me leave to do things around here my way."

The old man pulled up suddenly, his horse almost foundering under his rough handling. Cole reined in, also. His father looked at him.

"Damnit, son! As long as I live this land is mine! I don't propose to hand over either my land or my responsibilities to any other person, not even to my son. Now let's get on with this business."

The man's ire was aroused, Cole realized, his flinty blue eyes charged with passion. Delmar Randall was known throughout the Wyoming Territory as a hard man to tangle with, a lord of the high country who had never lost a battle, a poker game, or an acre of land since he rode up from Texas twenty-five years before beside a long line of straggly, lean-flanked longhorns.

Cole shrugged in weary resignation. "All right, pa. Just let me do the talking. This U.S. Marshal is not one bit frightened of you, but if you roar too loud, he just might do something foolish."

Cole's father patted the butt of his Colt. "Let him try," he said. "It'll be the last thing that fool toady does."

Cole sighed and urged his horse to a canter until he had caught up with Mike. The ramrod was grinning. He winked at Cole, then nodded respectfully to Cole's father as the man pulled up alongside them.

"There's two riders and a buggy crossing the flat," the ramrod told Cole's father. "Looks like Marshal Poole and that new deputy of his, Danny Larn."

The old man nodded and peered contemptuously out from under his frosted eyebrows, his eyes narrowing as he concentrated on the buggy following them.

Cole watched the two riders also, then turned his attention to the buggy. He had no doubt who was in it. The squat, bulky figure of Maxwell Harris was a familiar one to him—especially the nervous way the man flicked the reins. Harris preferred harnessed horses and buggy seats to the antic roll and pitch of a saddle. A man who had never shaken his Eastern habits, he had simply never taken to the West, Cole realized, as he rode closer. He wondered if this was what made the banker so ruthless, so narrow in his perceptions.

At once Cole chided himself for this ungenerous thought. There was plenty of men born and bred in the West who were just as ruthless as Maxwell Harris. And many a townsman and certainly a great many sodbusters had come to regard Cole's father as a harsh, unrelenting law unto himself—just as harsh and just as unrelenting as Harris appeared to them now. Even now, Cole knew, the presence of Del Randall had a way of quieting a saloon or sobering a poker game.

But Del Randall was not a Maxwell Harris, Cole told himself. No, his father was as tough and as unflinching as ironwood, but he was fair. No man could dispute that.

As Cole watched, the banker suddenly pulled off the rough trail and guided his buggy toward a clump of cottonwoods on a rise to their right, leaving Marshal Poole and his deputy to ride on alone toward them.

Cole glanced at his father. The old man had caught Harris's maneuver and swore with fine precision. He had been looking forward to a meeting with the banker, Cole realized. He smiled, relieved. With Harris keeping out of it, the marshal and his deputy should be easier to handle.

The two lawmen were less than fifty yards away when they pulled up to wait for Cole and his party to reach them. As he rode closer, Cole studied the deputy sitting his horse beside Poole. He did not like what he saw.

The deputy's name was Danny Larn. He had arrived in Broken Bow by stage less than two weeks before—but Cole had already heard quite a bit about him. On his arrival he had left the stage expensively dressed, a gleaming pearl-handled Smith & Wesson laced, gunslick fashion, to his thigh. Two days later in The Lady Luck, poor Sam Bellows accidentally spilled whiskey on Larn's coat. Sam was a local hothead, always truculent in his cups. An argument followed and before anyone could step between them, both men reached for their guns. Larn's polished Smith & Wesson flashed from its holster, spitting lead. Sam was dead before he hit the floor, two neatly spaced holes in his shirt.

Thus had Danny Larn presented his credentials. He was another of the hired guns Harris was gathering around him and his reluctant toady, Marshal Poole. And this was the man who was today siding a U.S. Deputy Marshal.

They had ridden close enough now, Cole judged. He reined in a few yards from the deputy, noting the man's hooded eyes, his cold, emotionless expression. The line of his mouth was thin, and his blade of a nose hooked slightly over his pencil-thin mustache. There was a light in Larn's eyes that disturbed Cole. It reminded him of a rope-shy bronc, mean and unpredictable—and very dangerous.

Cole turned his attention to the U.S. Marshal. "Howdy, Poole."

The man shifted unhappily in his saddle. He didn't like this any more than Cole did. "Howdy, Cole. Guess you know why we're here."

Cole smiled thinly and indicated the cottonwoods where

4

Harris had pulled up with a nod of his head. "And so does Harris. He's got himself a ringside seat, looks like."

"Couldn't stop him from comin', Cole."

"Just so he stays over there—out of trouble."

"He will."

Poole's deputy glanced with irritation at the U.S. Marshal. "You goin' to get on with this, Poole?"

Poole shot him a glance. "Shut up, Larn."

Larn's face went white and as cold as death. But he swallowed the rebuke without a rejoinder.

Poole looked back at Cole. "I got a court order here, Cole, signed by Judge Warner enjoinin' you to drive your cattle off this land."

"This is Circle C land, Poole. We're not getting off."

"It's railroad land, Cole," Poole said patiently. "You know that. You knew that long ago."

Cole's father spoke up then. "Serve that court order on the cattle, Poole."

Poole showed sudden exasperation. He chucked his hat back off his forehead. "You can't fight the government, Cole."

"Sure, we can."

"How?"

"By fightin' Harris."

"It ain't Harris alone you're fighting."

"Sure, it is, Poole," said Cole's father coldly.

"No, it ain't. It's the whole damned company—and the government, too. They's the ones gave all this land to the railroad. That's the law, Cole. And you can't go against the law."

"That the law sittin' beside you?" asked Mike Gunnison. The Circle C ramrod had been watching Larn closely.

"I can't help him, damnit!"

"No, you can't," said Cole succinctly. "Seems to me that's the point, Poole."

"What the hell do you mean by that?"

5

"Harris is the law in Broken Bow now—Harris and his railroad. He's got you in his pocket, Poole."

"I resent that, Cole," Poole said heavily.

"Then stop running errands for Harris."

"I ain't running errands for Harris, damnit! This is the law. Either buy this land from the railroad or get your herds off it."

"At thirty dollars an acre?"

Poole frowned unhappily. The price, he knew, was outrageous.

"Don Willard promised us we could buy this land back from the railroad at two-fifty to three dollars an acre when I settled here," Cole's father said. "That was the terms and we shook on it."

"You got that in writing, old man?" Larn asked, the trace of a smile on his lean, polished face.

Cole's father bristled at Larn's tone. "A handshake was sufficient for me, sir. And for Don Willard. An honest man needs nothing more in this country."

"Or a fool."

"You callin' me a fool, sir?"

Del Randall's face had gone deep red so that his frosted brows stood out in bold relief. He seemed ready to leap the breach that separated him from the deputy.

"Pa!" Cole said sharply. "I'll handle this."

Cole's father glanced at him. He seemed about to utter a sharp rebuke to his son. But then his shoulders sagged and he relaxed. Head still high, his seamed face grim, he nodded to Cole. "All right, Cole."

Poole blew out his cheeks in relief and fixed Cole with his gaze. He was a heavy man who had long since lost his appetite for long rides and sleeping under the stars. His marshal's badge had given him a license to put on girth and sleep in soft beds. It was easy to see why Harris had brought in help. Poole's cutting edge had been considerably dulled by town life. But he was still a tough man—and a fair one.

"Don Willard's dead," Poole said reasonably, "and he died with him and his railroad bankrupt—and still forty miles out of Broken Bow. It's Harris's group that owns the Northern & Central now—and there ain't no way in hell you're going to be able to change that."

"We'll see," said Cole.

"Damnit, Cole!"

"No, Poole. Damn Harris."

"You can't fight the railroad!"

"Watch us."

"There's no *way!*"

"Harris has his lawyers, we'll get ours."

"You any idea how much that'll cost? You might as well pay the thirty dollars an acre."

"You forget, Poole," Cole's father said. "We respect this land too much to let Harris bring in his hordes to settle on it. The soil in this high country is too thin for farming. Plowing this land will only kill the grass that grows on it. Soon enough these nesters will be starving for water and will end up killing my beef to live. They'll turn this country into a waste of barbed wire and bare ground."

"But that ain't the point, Del," Poole said. "This ain't your land! It's the railroad's."

Larn spoke up then, his voice scathing in its calculated contempt. "Come on, Poole. You've got a court order. Serve it! You going to let this tired old man and his whelp stall you here all day?"

In that instant Cole knew why Larn had come along. He was there to goad either Cole or his father into some rash action. Before Cole could react, however, and blunt the cut of Larn's words, Gunnison jumped in, furious at the way Larn had referred to Cole and his father.

"Watch your tongue, mister," the ramrod said, his voice menacing. As he spoke, he let his hand drop to his thigh.

Larn caught the motion—and its significance. Cole saw the thin trace of a smile on Larn's face as he swung his attention to Gunnison, his own right hand falling to his thigh.

"Well, now. The ramrod to the rescue, is it? You looking after those two, are you? Now just what makes you think you're up to the job, mister?"

"Gunnison," said Cole sharply. "Don't let this gunslick rile you. He's doing it deliberate. Just sit back and let me handle this."

Larn's hooded eyes flicked a glance in Cole's direction. Then he looked back to Gunnison. He evidently felt he had an easy mark in the ramrod, and he didn't want to pass up the opportunity. "That's right," Larn said, smiling. "Do as you're told, Gunnison. Back off."

"That's enough of that!" snapped Poole.

"All right," said Larn, smiling coldly. "I'll stop, Marshal. I wouldn't want to hurt the ramrod." Larn looked back at Gunnison. "I reckon you ain't got one-half the sand this tired old man and his whelp has. Sure, I'll leave you be, Gunnison. But you better keep your foul mouth shut from now on."

"Damn you!" Gunnison cried, his voice shaking with sudden fury. "Damn you to hell!"

As he spoke, he drew his iron. But with a pure, undiluted joy that shocked Cole, Larn drew his gleaming Smith & Wesson in one single effortless draw that beat Gunnison by a full two or three seconds. Larn's gun roared and Gunnison slipped back off his horse, glancing over at Cole with startled eyes, his hand clutching his side.

Both Cole and his father went for their guns. Furious at what Larn had done, Poole drew his revolver and swung at Larn. Larn ducked low. Poole missed. He never got a chance to swing at Larn again as the deputy shot him point-blank in the chest. As the marshal slid lifelessly out of his saddle, Larn dismounted. Using his horse as a shield, he got off a quick snap at Cole. Cole felt Larn's bullet pile into his empty holster. The violence of the round pulled

Cole sideways with such force that his shot went wild. He tried to get another shot off at the deputy, but the close gunplay had spooked his horse.

It reared with a screaming whinny and Cole toppled back out of his saddle, coming down with numbing force on his right shoulder. He lost his grip on his six-gun and looked dazedly up as his father fired furiously down at the dodging, grinning deputy. One quick clean shot from Larn followed the old man's flurry and Cole saw his father slam back, a blossoming darkness in the suit coat where it covered his left shoulder.

By that time Cole's senses had returned well enough for him to scramble across the ground for his six-gun. But even as he raised it to fire at Harris's hired gun, he saw the fellow swing his horse around and mount on the run. Bending low over the cantle, he galloped off, sending one last bullet in their direction before he was out of range.

Cole glanced up at his father. The old man was holding on tightly to the saddle horn, his face frozen into a mask of frustration, his head down. Mike Gunnison was sitting up and shaking his head, his right hand trying to stem the flow of blood that pulsed from the wound in his left side just below the rib cage. His face looked almost blue, his eyes dim, uncomprehending.

But all Cole could think of was that his father was safe. His wound was superficial. Nothing vital had been hit or the man would not still be in his saddle. Cole got to his feet and reached out for the bridle to his father's horse.

"You all right, pa?" he asked.

"The son-of-a-bitch is going to have it all his own way now!" Cole's father said, his voice filled with a frustrated torment. "It's his game now. He's got all the cards! You see that, Cole?"

"Sure, pa!" Cole said, hoping to quiet the old man. "Now take it easy. Let me help you down."

"He's over there now watching, gloating. Harris! That

damned buzzard's waiting now to pick our bones!"

With a furious oath, Cole's father yanked on his reins, dragging the bridle out of Cole's grasp. Without a look back at Cole, the old man spurred his mount past Cole and charged across the flat toward the cottonwoods where Harris still sat in his buggy, waiting.

Maxwell Harris had watched everything with mounting satisfaction. When he had noticed how long it was taking for the marshal to serve the court order, he could not help from emitting a low chuckle. The longer it took Poole, the more time that gave his man Larn to raise hell with Del Randall. What Harris was hoping for was an incident of some kind that would put that arrogant son-of-a-bitch on the defensive at last.

Even so, the sudden explosion of gunfire took the banker by surprise. When he saw Gunnison, then Poole slide from their horses and saw Larn exchange fire with Cole and Del Randall, he jumped to his feet in order to see more clearly. As abruptly as it had begun, the gunfire ceased and Harris saw Larn galloping off, flinging back one parting shot as he rode.

Harris sat back down, an exultant cry trembling in his throat. Cole and his father had played into his hands! By resisting the serving of this court order, they were outside the law. If in addition that temporizing fool, the marshal, was dead in the bargain . . . ! But that was too much to hope for. Enough for one day had been accomplished. Harris took up his reins.

Before he could flick them, he saw Del Randall, still astride his mount, spur suddenly away from his son and the others and start across the flat toward him. The first thing Harris felt was fear. It clutched at his entrails like a cold hand.

The old fool was shouting as he rode. As Harris heard the faint shouts, the invective, he remembered enough to still his fear—to replace it then with the pent-up fury he himself had nursed all these years. He reached down at his feet and picked up the double-barreled shotgun that waited there. It was a Greener, ten gauge, loaded with number eight buckshot.

Randall was close enough now to begin firing. He got off a wild shot and Harris crouched lower in his seat. The round snapped a hole in the buggy's top. Randall kept coming. He was shouting still, swaying crookedly in the saddle, his lean, plowed face distorted with rage. He fired again. This time the slug buried itself in the cushion beside Harris.

Harris felt no fear now, only elation. He had the mad sense that he was invulnerable, charmed. His medicine was working; Randall's was not. Harris stood up and brought the shotgun to his shoulder. Over the two barrels he caught the startled look on Randall's face, the sudden concern. The man appeared to waver in the sights as he started to pull his horse to the right. Harris tracked him effortlessly, waited, then fired both barrels.

A powerful, yet invisible hand swept Randall off his horse, knifing him, turning him, stopping him with the force of a solid object. If he had ridden into a low-hanging branch, he would not have been halted any more abruptly. The horse, nostrils flaring, galloped on without its rider and Harris dropped the Greener into the bottom of the buggy and snatched up his reins.

As Harris snapped his whip over the backs of his plunging team, he glanced down at Del Randall's sprawled body. One glimpse was enough for him. The old cattleman was on his back, his arms flung wide, and his six-gun still clutched miraculously in his right hand—his head and shoulders bright with gleaming ribbons of blood, with the raw look and texture of a newly slaughtered side of beef hanging in a barn.

Only it was worse than that.

From the way in which the head lay in relation to the shoulders, it was clear that the buckshot had decapitated Del Randall.

Shuddering involuntarily, Harris whipped his horses in a sudden, mindless frenzy. All he wanted now was to flee this horror—to find sanctuary, as he always had, behind the massive walls of his bank in Broken Bow.

Two

COLE REMAINED outside in the rain to thank Preacher
Weems as the rest of the burial party filed past them into
the ranchhouse.

Weems stood before his buggy, his hat in his hand while
the pelting rain plastered his thinning hair down upon his
narrow skull. The man kept his large, mournful eyes averted
as he spoke to Cole.

". . . and so, Cole, just try and think of it as God's will.
If you can, I mean."

"Thank you, Preacher," said Cole. "I'll try to remember
that."

"And you won't be doing nothing foolish now?"

"Of course not, Preacher. You better get up inside that
buggy before you get drowned."

Weems slapped his soggy hat down upon his head and

stepped up into the buggy and snatched up the reins with his large, bony hands. He cast one last mournful look down at Cole, then lifted the heavy reins and slapped his horses into motion.

Cole watched the man disappear into the sheets of rain and shook his head wearily. Preacher meant all right, he knew. But he wished somehow that a man built to a different scale than Preacher Weems had spoken over the dead body of his father. As it was, there was an air of incompleteness about the business—a haunting sense of waste.

He turned abruptly and mounted the low porch and pushed into the ranchhouse. Striding through the huge living room, he found everyone in the kitchen.

Bill Graham was slouched in the chair he had pulled up to the huge oak table, a bottle of Irish whiskey in his right hand, a beaten, almost stunned look in his eyes. The owner of the Box W had known Cole's father since before Cole's birth. The man had lost more than a friend; he had lost what amounted to a brother. Cole had known brothers who were not as close as Bill Graham and Del Randall had been.

Cole's hired men were keeping away from the table and the almost palpable sorrow that hung about Graham. Pete and Gus stood by the sink, talking together softly, unhappily. Fiddle Twofoil was stoking the huge wood stove and had already placed a pot of coffee onto it. The smell of the coffee was just about driving out the dampness that hung in the room. Gunnison was propped in a chair beside the stove, the foreman's pale, drawn face slack now in exhaustion. Cole had been astonished—and touched—at the man's endurance by the graveside. He had stood alone, unaided, tears coursing unashamedly down his face.

Consuelo was not in the kitchen. Neither was Linda, Bill's daughter. Without needing to be told, Cole knew Linda was in the bedroom comforting Consuelo.

Bill looked up as Cole entered the kitchen and indicated the bottle in his hand with a bitter glance. "First time in my life good whiskey don't have no more effect on me than drinking water."

Cole nodded wearily and sat down across from Bill, sweeping off his soaked hat and swinging it to rid the brim of the moisture. He glanced over at Fiddle. "That coffee smells good, Fiddle."

"Be ready in a jiffy, Cole."

Fiddle almost visibly swelled with appreciation that Cole had noticed his efforts with the coffee. He bustled eagerly over to the cupboard and began hauling down cups and saucers.

Cole looked back at Bill. The man was drinking from the bottle, punishing himself with enormous gulps. Cole reached over and placed a hand on his wrist. "Go easy, Bill. We've got to talk."

Bill blinked his pale blue eyes and nodded briskly. He stoppered the bottle and placed it down heavily on the table before him. His thin, sandy hair barely covered his head so that he might as well have been bald. A dark tan-line circled his forehead just above his eyebrows. Like most men who had spent a lifetime outdoors astride a horse, he looked almost naked and sadly diminished under a roof and without a hat. He turned his seamed, weathered face upon Cole.

"We got to get him, Cole."

"You mean Harris?"

"You goddamn right I mean Harris—and that pack of gunslicks at his heels."

This is what Cole had expected from Bill. "I don't think so, Bill," he said quietly, firmly.

"Well, damnit! Why not? You saw what that money-lender did to your pa!"

Cole nodded patiently. "Harris has gone too far this time. And that puts it squarely in the hands of the law."

"Law? What law? You shot down the only law we had left in Broken Bow."

"No, I didn't, Bill. I thought I told you what happened."

Gunnison spoke up then, his face gray with pain. "Like Cole said, Bill, it was Danny Larn shot the marshal. I saw it clear as day. Forget what else you heard."

Bill shrugged, as if to say "Have it your way." It was plain to Cole that Bill simply discounted Cole's earlier account of the confrontation without giving the matter a second thought. And now he simply refused to believe what Gunnison had just told him.

Cole wondered then how many others preferred to believe as Bill did—that Cole and his father were the ones who had forced the issue and shot down the Deputy U.S. Marshal. At once Cole found himself remembering the cool, unsympathetic stares of those townspeople who had witnessed him bringing in Poole's body yesterday. At the time he had refused to pay much attention to their manner, so preoccupied had he been with the awesome finality of his father's death. But now in his mind's eye he saw once again those cold faces. Yes, they must have all believed what Bill did. It was natural, Cole realized, for them to accept such a version, especially where Del Randall and the Circle C were involved.

"Gunnison's telling the truth, Bill," said Cole firmly. "Just forget whatever you heard and what you figure happened. I told you how it was."

"Aw, hell, Cole. You think I care if you shot the son-of-a-bitch? You don't have to tell *me* no fairy tales. The point is, what are we going to do to stop Harris and that damn railroad of his? That's what your pa wanted, Cole. That's why he died. You can't let Harris get away with it. Your pa sure as hell wouldn't stand by like this if that were your body out there under the cottonwoods. He wouldn't let the law do his job for him. He knew too damn much about the law to trust a single judge or lawyer. Buzzards, all of them. That's what your pa thought—and he was right!"

16

Cole took a deep breath. "Bill, now you listen to me and listen good. I don't give a damn what you think my father would have done. I'm in charge here now. And I say we stay within the law. That's the way I want it, and that's the way it is going to be."

Bill's flushed face went ashen. This was the first time Del Randall's quiet son had ever talked to him like this. Cole read this thought in Bill's expression. He leaned back in his chair and watched the outrage blossom furiously in Bill Graham's face. And just as quickly fade.

Bill's shoulders slumped wearily. He reached for the bottle. "Okay, Cole. Forget your pa. Do it your way. So what's next?"

"I'm going to wait for the new Deputy U.S. Marshal to be appointed. He's going to want to know what happened. Mike and I are eyewitnesses. We saw what Danny Larn did—and Larn is Harris's man. Meanwhile, I'm going to see if I can organize the rest of the cattlemen in the valley. We need to pool our resources and get ourselves a good lawyer to fight Harris. I figure Eliot Trace might do nicely. He's honest, and I like the man. I'm counting on you, Bill. If the Box W and the rest of us can stick together, we can delay Harris long enough to make him want to cut his losses and settle with us. I think we can do it. But we've got to stick together."

"Hell, Cole, you know you ain't got to ask." Bill drank from the bottle and wiped his mouth with the back of his forearm. "Box W and Circle C have always rode together."

"Thanks, Bill. That means I shouldn't have too much trouble with the others now. Maybe they didn't all love my father—but they at least respected him."

Bill looked at Cole sharply. "Yes, sir, Cole. They sure as hell did."

Cole leaned back in his chair, relieved. Keeping Bill Graham from blowing matters sky high had been his first concern. When Fiddle saw the brief lull in the conversation, he quickly placed coffee mugs down on the table and went back for the coffee. In the waiting silence Cole thought he heard the steady pounding of a horse's hooves above the sound of the rain. He leaned back in his chair and turned his head to listen.

Abruptly he rose to his feet and headed for the kitchen door. He flung it open. It was raining in great driving sheets now. The bare ground of the compound seemed to boil under the impact of the slashing downpour. Through the heavy, shifting curtains of rain came what looked like Cy Reese, the Box W's sole ranchhand. His yellow slicker gleamed in the late-afternoon light. Cy kept pushing his horse without letup until he had reached the porch hitch rails.

"Over here, Cy!" Cole called from the open doorway as Cy swung down from his saddle.

Cole stepped out of the doorway to let Cy in. The man stomped into the kitchen, his slicker gleaming brightly as the rain poured off it. Cole looked across the room at his two hands standing by the stove.

"One of you might take care of Cy's horse."

"I'll go, Cole," Ames said at once, and went looking for his slicker.

Bill Graham spoke to his ranchhand. "There's hot coffee over there on the stove, Cy. Help yourself."

"Thanks, Bill," the man said, swinging his hat.

"And step out of that slicker before you drown us all," Bill added with a grin.

"Sure," Cy said nervously, glancing with a frown toward Cole.

"What is it, Cy?" Cole asked. "You act like a man who's got bad news—the kind of news he ain't so anxious to pass on."

The fellow's small, wizened face screwed up into what passed for a grin. He was too concerned to laugh. As he

18

shrugged out of the slicker, he said, "That's about it, I guess, Cole."

Bill moved impatiently in his chair. "Damnit, man! Out with it then! What's up?"

Cy turned to his boss. "I just came from town. Danny Larn's the new Deputy U.S. Marshal. The telegram came this afternoon from the lieutenant governor. It was addressed to Judge Warner. Harris is behind it, looks like. Larn'll be sworn in official tomorrow. Larn says as soon as he is, he'll be out to arrest Cole and Mike."

"Arrest us?" Cole asked sharply.

Cy turned back to Cole and nodded unhappily. "For the murder of Marshal Poole."

Bill looked at Cole. "Now that's somethin' none of us figured. Danny Larn the new Deputy U.S. Marshal. That son-of-a-bitchin' Harris didn't waste no time at all, did he?"

"Like he had it all planned," Gunnison said softly from his chair. He moved painfully, trying to get a comfortable position.

"Go get your coffee, Cy," said Cole. "And thanks."

Like a man who has just dropped an enormous burden, Cy hurried over to the stove where Fiddle had already poured Cy a cup of coffee. Cole looked across the room at his ramrod.

"Looks like the law is Danny Larn now, Mike."

"You can't let him take you, Cole."

"Not now, I can't. Not before I've had a chance to organize the rest of the cattlemen—and talk to Eliot Trace."

"Light out, Cole," Gunnison said. "I'll go in town tomorrow and give myself up. That ought to satisfy them for now."

"You mean toss 'em a bone."

"I want to go in anyway, Cole. This wound's not getting any better and I think Doc Wilder should take another look at it. If Larn arrests me, you can bail me out."

"That's right. But I don't want to take any chances with Larn. He's a killer."

"I can handle that son-of-a-bitch, Cole. I won't be so slow this time."

"You're a wounded man, Mike. Talk sense."

"I'll go in with him, Cole," said Pete.

"Me too," said Fiddle.

Cole thought a moment, then shook his head at Fiddle. "You'll be needed here, Fiddle. Pete will do."

Cole looked back at Gunnison. "You'll be going into Broken Bow the first thing in the morning. Go in without making any commotion. I just don't want you to give Larn any excuse at all. See Doc Wilder first, then Eliot Trace. If Larn locks you up, Trace should have you out on bail before the afternoon's out."

Mike got up from his chair wearily, grimacing from the effort.

"Right now I think I'll get me some shut-eye."

Fiddle and Pete went with Mike as he left the kitchen. Cole walked with the three as far as the kitchen doorway. He didn't like Gunnison's color. What had appeared at first glance to have been nothing more serious than a flesh wound in his side had turned ugly overnight. If it were not for the rain, Cole would have insisted that Mike start for town this afternoon. Gus Ames met them halfway across the compound and the four men slogged through the downpour to the bunkhouse. Cole watched them go for a moment, then turned back to the kitchen.

Linda was standing by her father's chair.

Cole walked toward her. "How's Consuelo?"

Linda shook her head wearily. "She won't say a thing, Cole. She just sits in that rocker and looks out at the cottonwoods."

"I'm sure she appreciated your being with her, Linda."

"I hope so, Cole."

20

Her father turned to look at her. "Danny Larn is the new Deputy U.S. Marshal, Linda. What do you think of that?"

Linda frowned in sudden alarm at Cole. "Danny Larn, Cole?"

Cole nodded.

Linda slumped into a chair beside her father. She was a small, fragile-appearing girl with thick auburn hair she wore in pigtails wound in a crown upon her head. Her cheekbones were prominent, finely modeled, her eyebrows pencil-thin. Combined with the delicate features, her wide, mischievous brown eyes and a perky, upturned nose gave her an almost elfin appearance. She and Cole had been neighbors since childhood. It had always been taken for granted they would marry. Cole felt very protective toward her, since they had grown up more like kid-sister, big-brother than lovers. Recently Cole had become somewhat uncertain as to how to regard Linda, especially now that her slight nineteen-year-old figure had begun to fill out.

"Thing is," said Bill, "we can't afford to rile Danny Larn none. Since now he's the law. Ain't that right, Cole?"

There was more than a trace of sarcasm in Bill's voice, but Cole chose to ignore it. He sat down at the table and pulled toward him his cold cup of coffee. Sipping it, he nodded his agreement. "That's right, Bill. And it don't take much at all to rile his kind. Pete and Mike better make as little commotion as possible when they go in."

Bill rubbed his face harshly in sudden exasperation at Cole's response, but forced himself to say nothing. Linda saw at once her father's state and jumped into the conversation in an effort to save the situation.

"What are *you* going to do, Cole?"

He told her briefly of his intention to stay one jump ahead of Larn until he had spoken to the rest of the ranchers in the valley and convinced them to throw in with the Circle C and the Box W. The trouble was, he pointed out to her, this meant he was going to be running from the law for a while.

Linda smiled at him. "You know you're always welcome at the Box W, Cole."

Cole grinned. "Even if I'm riding the owl-hoot trail?"

"Now, damnit, you know you ain't even got to ask," Bill said emphatically.

"That's mighty generous of you, Bill."

"Nothing more'n I'd say to your pa," Bill said, downing his coffee. He glanced over at Linda. "You better say good-bye to Cole while Cy and I harness up the team."

She nodded to her father and smiled self-consciously across the table at Cole as her father got a little unsteadily to his feet. He grabbed for his hat, slapped it onto his head, and walked after Cy Reese out of the kitchen. As the door slammed shut behind the two men, Cole met Linda's gaze.

"Thanks for coming, Linda."

"How do you feel, Cole?"

"This place will sure be lonely now," he said. "A man who filled it up pretty well is gone. It's hard for me to believe that."

"I imagine so," she agreed gently.

"Just me and Consuelo now." It sounded idiotic, the way he said it, and he saw Linda blush slightly, as if she had been expecting him to say something entirely different.

At once Cole knew with certainty what Linda was thinking: it was time now for them to think of filling the sudden emptiness of this big ranchhouse with their laughter, the warmth of their love. And what Linda wanted now—what she needed—was some sign from him, some word that their marriage was what Cole too was hoping for.

He finished the cold coffee quickly and got to his feet. "We'd better wait out on the front porch," he told her, without meeting her eyes. "Where's your slicker?"

"It's in Consuelo's bedroom. I'll get it."

Cole watched Linda leave the kitchen, then got up from

the table and strode through the hall and out onto the porch. The rain drumming on the porch roof effectively blotted out his troubled thoughts, his confusion about Linda.

There was a distant solemnity in Linda's manner as she said good-bye and something in her eyes that told Cole not to worry, that she understood and was not disheartened. He waved to her as she ducked through the rain to the waiting buggy. Cy helped her up onto the seat and they drove off through the steady rain, Cy's unsaddled horse on a lead behind the buggy.

As they disappeared beyond the gate, Cole looked toward the cottonwoods where his father lay next to his mother's grave. The man had come to earth almost twenty years after Cole's mother, but he was beside her now—gone to join her as suddenly and as violently as he had done everything else in his crowded life. Cole took a deep breath, pulled his hat down securely, and stepped off the porch, heading for the cottonwoods.

The trees were leafing out as spring came on and offered Cole some protection from the rain's lash as he stood before the mound of fresh brown earth that covered his father's coffin. He found himself trying to remember his father's face, his voice—to recreate in some way the man's enormous vitality, his unquenchable thirst for life. He had dominated Cole's life the same way he had managed to dominate any room he entered, any horse he rode, any saloon he favored with his trade. But a picture of his father would not grow in his mind.

That Cole was diminished sorely by his father's death, he knew with an aching certainty. But he knew also that he would surely be able to survive without his father. Of that there was no question—and indeed, an errant, fugitive part of him was relieved to be at last out from under the enormous shadow his father had always cast.

But the moment Cole thought this, he reacted with sorrow and shame at such an ungenerous thought. How then *did* he feel?

The answer came with a rush. He would miss his father. Terribly. There was much in the man he could never emulate. But he had loved the man, and his father had loved him. At last Cole let his emotions go, let them take whatever course they would. The unashamed tears came now, freely spent. He let the rain and the genuine sorrow he felt at his father's death wash over, cleansing him. . . .

Cole knocked softly on Consuelo's door, then pushed it open gently. The old woman still rocked in the same chair where Linda had left her, her gaze still intent on the cottonwood grove—and, Cole imagined, the fresh new grave within it.

Not a feature on her brown face, wrinkled as a walnut, altered the slightest at his entrance. Nothing about her gave any indication that she had heard him enter. But Cole understood perfectly. Her soul was capable of vast concentration as she listened at times like this to the voices of her people's vanished gods; yet it had never prevented her from hearing him. She had always been at his side when he needed her—either for comfort or for chastisement.

She wore her thick, still jet-black hair in a tight bun on the top of her head, giving it the appearance of a small, comical hat. Around her broad shoulders she still wore the dark shawl she had used for the funeral. Her buckskin dress, heavily fringed about the hem, was still soaking from the rain; the battered, hand-tooled riding boots she took such pride in were still caked with the mud of the graveside.

Consuelo was not a full-blooded Indian. The Sioux had purchased her mother, a well-born Mexican, from Comancheros. Consuelo still kept about her neck the locket her mother had left her; within it was her mother's faded picture. Cole's father had given her the name Consuelo when he had found it engraved on the back of the locket.

Delmar Randall had never married Consuelo. It would have made him a squaw man. But within a year after he had brought Consuelo from the Sioux reservation in Rimrock Basin to serve as his housekeeper, she had moved in to comfort his bed as well. Cole's father had never bothered to explain this to Cole, knowing undoubtedly that at Cole's age at the time there could be no satisfactory explanation. When Cole had grown older, he found he required none. Consuelo had become a vital member of the family, an efficient wife to his father and to Cole a mother who always gave him the room he needed, not only to secure his own triumphs, but also to make his own mistakes.

Cole could still remember the impassive efficiency with which Consuelo set his broken leg and bound it securely in a splint after he had disobeyed his father and tried to ride the outlaw bronc they owned at the time. Her eyes had revealed the pride she felt in his daring and the amusement too at his chagrin. She had uttered not a word of reproof as she worked over him, and had let him be the one to tell his father.

"Consuelo," Cole said gently, placing his right hand on her shoulder.

She moved her head and looked up at him, her black eyes impassive, and stopped rocking.

"This is your home, Consuelo. Always. As long as I live."

There was not the slightest change in her expression, though her eyes seemed to grow deeper.

"You were a good wife to my father," he told her. "And a growing hellion like me couldn't have asked for a better mother."

She spoke then. "I stay all these years—not for him. For you." Then with a surprising display of emotion, she reached up and placed her right hand over his. "Now you are a man."

Cole bent and kissed her on the forehead.

Consuelo released his hand. "Good-bye, Cole."

Cole frowned, vaguely troubled. "Good night, Consuelo. Don't worry about the house. Get some sleep if you can."

Consuelo nodded, then resumed her rocking—but slower now, almost as if she had been waiting for Cole to come in and speak to her. As Cole pulled the door shut, he looked back and saw that she was once more gazing out at the cottonwoods, only now, he realized, there was an upright, almost proud, tilt to her head.

Cole was emotionally drained. He went to the kitchen window and looked across the yard at the bunkhouse. Through the rain he could see the bunkhouse windows bright with the glow of lanterns. He thought then of Mike Gunnison.

It would be a long ride for Mike tomorrow into Broken Bow, and Cole suddenly decided he had better ride a good part of the way with Pete and his ramrod before starting north to see the other cattlemen. Just to be on the safe side. With Danny Larn sporting a Deputy U.S. Marshal's badge, all of them—as Bill Graham had pointed out with poisonous sarcasm—had to be especially careful.

Three

DANNY LARN pulled up so swiftly the Spanish bit he was using sawed cruelly on his dun's mouth. The animal reared slightly in discomfort. Larn paid it no heed as he swore with deep, passionate frustration. The four riders with him crowded up onto the ridge and pulled to a halt also.

"Damn!" said Miles Crocket, his long bony face twisting as he fought back—then gave in to—a sudden, wracking cough. "There goes Randall." He wiped his mouth with a bandanna he kept in the side pocket of his heavy deerskin jacket.

"You want us to split up and go after him, Danny?"

"No. Better we stick together."

Danny watched the lone horseman climb the far ridge, then vanish beyond it, heading north. Then Danny turned his attention to the rutted dirt road that wound along the

27

floor of the valley. A farm wagon—toylike at this distance—was heading toward Broken Bow. A wounded man was lying on his back in the wagon bed while a cowhand in a battered Stetson drove the two-horse team. The fellow lying in the bed of the wagon was most likely Mike Gunnison. When Cole brought in Poole's body, there had been mention of Gunnison's condition. Evidently it had worsened and the ramrod was being taken in to Broken Bow to see Doc Wilder. Cole Randall had ridden part of the way to insure the ramrod's safety from road agents and such like. Danny smiled.

"We'll just see to Gunnison first," he told Miles. "Seems like I ought to finish what I start."

Danny put his horse down the slope, the rest following carefully as they gave their horses their heads and let them pick their own way down the steep incline. Danny was in the lead—the rest of the riders pulling in behind him—when they reached the valley floor and started at a fast run across the sage-covered flat toward the road.

They were coming up on the wagon from behind when the driver of the team heard the pound of their hoofbeats and turned to look back. Startled at what he saw, the man snapped the reins over his team and urged his horses to greater speed. Danny waved his men into an enveloping line past him. As the four riders drew abreast of the wagon, Miles cut in close to the horse closest to him, grabbed its halter, and yanked it back viciously. The horse almost went down. The cowpoke hauled back on the reins and brought the team to a sudden, hock-rattling halt.

Danny rode up to the wagon. As the fellow reached back behind the seat for a rifle, Danny casually drew his gun. The cowpoke forgot the rifle. Danny looked at Gunnison. The ramrod looked like he had been flung down a mountainside. He was struggling wordlessly to prop his back against the wagon's sideboard.

Danny looked at the wagon driver. "Know who I am, cowboy?"

"Danny Larn."

"*Marshal* Danny Larn, cowboy." Danny smiled and looked at Gunnison. "How do you feel after that ride, ramrod?"

Mike Gunnison just glared at Danny.

Danny laughed again and holstered his six-gun. Then he folded his arms over the pommel and leaned a little closer. "Looks like you're bleeding some. Someone shoot you, Gunnison?"

"You son-of-a-bitch," Gunnison said softly.

"If you was armed you wouldn't talk like that to the law."

"Well, I'm not armed. But I sure as hell wished I was."

"Of course you do. You're a brave man."

Danny looked at the cowpoke. "What's your name, friend?"

"I ain't your friend."

"What's your name?"

"Pete Anton."

"How long you been working for this four-flusher, Pete?"

"He ain't no four-flusher!"

"You calling me a liar?"

Anton frowned quickly and looked around at the circle of grinning faces. At once he realized what Danny was up to. He swallowed and his complexion lost its color. His tongue darted out to lick suddenly dry lips. "All I'm saying is he ain't no four-flusher. He's a damn good ramrod. And fair."

"Now ain't that touching. What a loyal, devoted servant you are, and that's a fact."

The sarcasm stung, but the cowboy refused to let himself be provoked any further. "We're on our way into Broken

29

Bow," he said. "What do you want with us?"

"It ain't you, cowpoke. It's this here ramrod of yours. I got a warrant for his arrest." As he said this, Danny could not help smiling.

"We're already on our way into Broken Bow," Gunnison managed through pain-tight lips. "I got to see a doctor. Save your damn warrant. You don't need it, Larn."

Larn looked at Miles then, a swift glance that told the man all he needed to know; then he glanced back down at the wounded man propped up painfully in the bed of the wagon. "That's right. I guess we don't need no warrant at that. Not as long as you're willing to come peaceable."

Obviously relieved, Pete Anton nodded vigorously. "Well, that's what we aim to do, ride into Broken Bow peaceable."

"Do you now?" Danny glanced again at Miles.

"Yes, damn it. You heard me." Then Anton saw the riders moving their mounts closer, their faces hardening— a look of pure malice on not a few of them.

"I wish," Danny said menacingly, "that you would stop arguing with me. All I want is for you two to come quietly and not give me and my deputies here any trouble."

"What the hell do you mean? I ain't arguin' with you!"

"There now," said Danny, shaking his head unhappily. "You just won't listen to reason, will you?" He removed his weapon from its holster and nodded quickly to Miles.

Miles spurred his horse close to the team, whipped off his hat, and slapped at the right-hand horse's face with it. The animal snorted in sudden panic and bolted, taking the other horse along with him. Roweling his horse with sudden fury, Miles drew his six-gun and fired just over the horses' heads. They swerved, maddened by fear, and plunged off the road. Pete Anton sawed frantically on the reins, but there was simply nothing he could do. He was too busy keeping himself on the narrow seat and hanging onto the reins even to curse at Miles.

Danny sat his horse and watched, the other riders staying back with him and grinning at the sight. After a moment Danny turned to them. "Let's go," he told them. "Time we finished this."

Galloping hard after the plunging wagon, Danny closed on it quickly, his men barely keeping up with him. Pete Anton was on his feet now, hanging on to the reins, his knees bent to absorb the shocks of the ride as the wagon jolted over the uneven ground. Behind him in the wagon bed Mike Gunnison's loose frame jumped and bucked convulsively with each violent bounce of the wagon, looking to Danny like an oversized rag doll with the stuffing about ready to come out. Danny's Smith & Wesson was still in his right hand. He sighted quickly on Pete Anton and fired. It was a tough shot, made even more so by the erratic bouncing of the wagon—the kind of challenge Danny liked. He saw the explosion of blood that appeared like a bud on the back of a cowpoke's neck as the cowboy let go the reins and with arms outflung peeled off the wagon seat.

In a moment Danny overtook the wagon. The horses had let up only slightly as they plunged on, driven by an ecstasy of fear. Danny looked down into the wagon bed.

Mike Gunnison appeared to have sprung a leak. His entire shirt front and vest were dark with blood. The jolting had opened up his wound nicely. The man was unconscious now, his face slack and stone-white. Roweling his horse savagely, Danny pulled abreast of the wagon, then galloped ahead until he was riding alongside Miles.

"Keep it going!" he cried. "Keep it going!"

Miles nodded and fired two more shots over the horses' heads, turning their panic into an eye-bulging frenzy.

Danny pulled up then, the rest of his riders doing the same. As he watched the wagon bouncing over the flat, he said to them, "Wait'll the wagon breaks up. That should finish Gunnison nicely." He shook his head solemnly. "If only that damn-fool cowpoke hadn't tried to outrun us, this

31

would never have happened. It's a damn shame, that's what it is."

The understanding between Danny and his men was faultless. The four men nodded soberly and each one allowed as how it sure was a pity.

The wagon with Miles still racing alongside it disappeared from sight into a shallow wash, then reappeared again on the far side. A moment later it was in among some rocks. Danny saw the wagon leaping crazily. Abruptly it lost a wheel. The axle dug into the ground. The wagon twisted violently to the right, then rose high into the air as the spooked horses pulled it on relentlessly.

Then Danny saw the body of Mike Gunnison hurtling high into the air as the wagon flipped. The body, twisting slowly in midair, came down hard among some rocks. Danny watched intently. The body did not stir—not that he had really expected it to.

One of the horses was foundering now as the wagon disintegrated. A second wheel went rolling away, leaping absurdly high as it bounded over the boulder-strewn flat.

Danny started his horse up then and took after the shattered wagon. He passed Gunnison's body without looking down at it. When he reached the wagon, one of the horses was down and kicking futilely at his traces; the other—head tossing, eyes wild—was standing beside it, blowing furiously. All that was left of the farm wagon was a wheelless, shattered hulk wedged securely between two boulders.

Miles was surveying the wreckage with some satisfaction, his bandanna held up to his mouth.

"Unhitch whichever horse is healthy," Danny told him. "We'll need it to take in what's left of these two damn fools."

Miles nodded and pocketed his bandanna as the rest of Danny's men pounded up.

"Help Miles," Danny told them.

Then Danny rode back to the spot where Gunnison lay

and looked down at what was left of the man. The ramrod had come down face first onto a large flat rock, then rolled lifelessly off it. He was resting now with his left arm twisted grotesquely under his body. The face was unrecognizable— a battered, purplish mess. Already flies were buzzing about it.

As Danny looked down at the dead man, he felt nothing. Only an appalling emptiness. No compassion. No sorrow. No anger. Nothing. At times like this the emptiness inside him seemed to yawn open prodigiously. What was wrong with him? He *knew* others felt things at times like this: exultancy, horror, exhilaration, revulsion—but *something*. Why was it impossible for him to feel anything—anything at all?

Irritated at the direction his thoughts were taking, Danny pulled his dun around and galloped across the flat toward his men.

He would wait until tomorrow to go after Cole. This was enough for one day. Danny thought then of Pauline's, and that dusky little wench she had brought in a couple of days ago. Young she was, and fresh. It looked like she might have a trace of Indian blood. Her eyes were sullen and smoky. He felt a surge of fire in his loins.

Well! Maybe he *could* feel something, after all! He sure as hell felt *that*. . . .

Maxwell Harris was sitting behind his desk, studying Friday's ledger. He was pleased at the increase in bank deposits. The rise was significant and Harris was certain he knew why. He was bringing the railroad—and prosperity—to Broken Bow. And, just as he had hoped, this in turn was bringing prosperity to his bank. If this rate of deposits continued, he would make it. No question at all of that.

There was a sharp knock on his door, and then one of his clerk's entered.

"Well?" Harris slammed shut the ledger.

"They just brought in Cole and his ramrod! They're dead, Mr. Harris. Both of them!"

Harris stood up. "You sure of this?"

"Danny Larn just pulled up in front of Stitch Anderson's with two bodies slung over a horse—and the horse had a Circle C brand!"

Harris brushed eagerly past the clerk, and left the bank. Once out on the sidewalk, he saw the crowd gathering in front of Stitch's barber shop, immense relief flooding him. It was not for need of a haircut that those two bodies were being left there; Anderson was also Broken Bow's undertaker.

It was over, he thought, as he hurried along the walk. As simple as that. Cole Randall and his ramrod were dead. And with Randall out of his way, there would be no more opposition from the other ranchers—no need to let them buy any of that land, no matter what that fool Willard had promised them. With that right of way his without any more controversy, there would be no need for further capitalization. He could purchase the rolling stock and hire the crews. Hell, they could be laying track before the month was out!

He shoved his way through the crowd. Stitch saw him and stepped aside. Doc Wilder—in his vest and shirtsleeves, his gray face sober—was examining the face of one of the men Larn had brought in. Harris felt suddenly sick. He could not tell if it was Cole's face or his ramrod's. It was not a pretty sight.

"Dead, all right," the doctor said to Stitch. "Took one hell of a spill, looks like. I'll sign the certificates and send them over." He turned then to walk back to his office.

"Well, Doc," Harris said, "that's what I call quick action. Looks like we got ourselves a U.S. Marshal, finally."

"You mean a murderer. It don't make any difference, him having a badge, Harris. He's still your hired gun."

The doctor's words were spoken loudly and clearly. There was not a pair of ears on either side of the street that did not hear the man.

Harris felt as if the doctor had struck him. He felt his face flush and glanced around for support. But every eye he met looked quickly away. Harris looked angrily back to the doctor.

"You got no call to say that, Doc. Damnit! Cole asked for this when he decided to shoot it out with Poole."

"Maybe so, but killing his ramrod and his cowhand isn't the way to bring Cole Randall in. You and your hired gun keep this up and we'll have a range war on our hands." As the doctor's words were spoken, there were several nods and a few who growled their assent.

"Wait a minute," said Harris. "You mean Cole isn't one of them two?"

"No, sir. He isn't. That's his ramrod and one of his cowpokes."

Harris was stunned. He looked around in sudden confusion and saw Danny Larn shoving his way through the crowd toward him, his insolent, immaculate features set in a cruel smile.

"Damnit, Larn!" Harris cried as the man pulled up in front of him. "What happened, anyway?"

"You want I should tell you out here?" The question was asked with an insolence that brought some laughter from the crowd.

"No, damnit! We'll go to your office."

Larn touched the brim of his gray Stetson in mock deference and stepped back to allow the banker to precede him through the crowd. Harris burst past the bystanders, his fury causing him to tremble as he walked. Harris realized then—though he was powerless to alter a thing—that he was acting ridiculously and causing anyone who looked upon him to think of him as a strutting peacock who had just had his feathers ruffled. Yet he did not slow down and indeed was almost running by the time he reached the marshal's office.

He ducked inside and whirled then to await Larn's leisurely arrival. Larn still had that cold smile on his face when he entered his office.

"I suggest you close the door," Harris said.

Larn did as he was told. Harris cleared his throat.

"Well? Let's have it," he snapped. "I sent you after Gunnison and Cole Randall. Where's Randall?"

"Gunnison was closer. It was more convenient to get Gunnison first. We'll go after Randall tomorrow."

"What do you mean, 'convenient'?"

Larn slipped into his chair behind his desk and looked up at the banker. "You want the truth or the way I'll be telling it?"

Harris moistened suddenly dry lips and slumped into a wooden chair by the desk. "The truth."

Larn told him—everything. He spared no details.

Harris nodded as Larn finished up, stirring uncomfortably. He reached into his vest pocket for a cigar and unwrapped it with unsteady hands. "So how are you going to tell it?"

"That when we came upon them, they fired at us and tried to outrun us with their wagon. That's when we fired at the cowpoke and killed him. And it was the jouncing in the back of the wagon and then him going flying that killed the ramrod. I figure that should match the doc's autopsy fairly well. He did bounce around some, and that's a fact."

"Yes," Harris said, lighting the cigar. "Yes, that should cover it nicely, Larn. The wagon is still out there. It will testify to the truth of your story, I am sure. But I doubt if there'll be any inquiry. I doubt that strongly."

"I didn't think there would be. But this way we're covered."

"It won't be so easy with Cole, you realize."

"Guess not."

"And it's Cole we've got to have, Larn. I can't have him stirring up those ranchers. Now, you've got that warrant—serve it."

Larn didn't answer. He just looked coolly at the banker, a thin, mocking trace of a smile on his polished, clean-shaven face. He had been on a horse most of the morning and from his own account had seen to the killing of two men—yet to Harris he appeared as neat and as clean as he must have looked when he rode out of Broken Bow that morning. There was something unsettling—unnatural even—about such fanatical cleanliness.

"I'll take care of Cole," Larn said finally. "Don't you worry none about that."

Harris got to his feet. "Good. Then I'll expect you to get your men together and ride out after Cole Randall this afternoon."

"I ain't going nowhere this afternoon," Larn said, smiling. "My boys are wettin' their whistle at the Lady Luck and I'm going to wake up one of Miss Pauline's girls."

Harris felt his face growing scarlet. "Now, you listen to me, Larn! It was my wire to the lieutenant governor that put that badge on your chest. I can take it off just as easily. I'll have no insolence from your kind!"

"From my kind, Mr. Harris?"

"Yes," Harris snapped angrily, "from your kind. You know what you are and I know what you are." Harris was surprised at his own recklessness—and pleased, too, at the way he was standing up to Larn.

"You ever kill a man, Harris? I mean besides using that shotgun on old Randall?"

"Now just what kind of a question is that?"

"I killed twenty-two men, Mr. Harris—including my father. And you know what? I never felt a thing—not a damn thing. Why do you think that is, Mr. Harris? You got any ideas on that?"

Harris was appalled at Larn's words—and at the cold,

almost maniacal gleam in his eyes as he spoke. It occurred to him then that he had really very little control over this killer he had brought in. Yes, he'd better use a little more discretion in his dealings with the man.

Harris took the cigar out of his mouth and noticed that his right hand was shaking slightly.

"No, Larn. I don't have any ideas on that, I'm afraid. But I'm sure those men deserved killing."

"Are you, now?"

"Yes. Of course."

"Most men deserve killing, Mr. Harris. I certainly do. And you, as well. Wouldn't you say?"

Harris moistened his dry lips. "I suppose you could say that."

"What did you feel when you killed old Randall?"

"I felt . . . very poorly for a while."

"Word was you got sick when you got home." Larn smiled.

"That's none of your business!"

"I don't get sick. You understand that, Mr. Harris?"

"Are . . . you threatening me?"

"I just don't like you to talk to me the way you done just now—like I was dirt. It reminds me of somebody."

"Somebody you . . . ?"

"That's right, Mr. Harris. Somebody I killed. I'm going to Pauline's this afternoon so I can feel better." Larn's eyes glittered. "I want to feel something for a change. Can you understand that?"

"Why . . . why don't you have a few drinks with your men?"

"I don't like to drink. It's a filthy habit—like smoking." He was looking at the cigar in Harris's right hand.

"All right, then. Tomorrow," Harris said, almost hastily. "If you go after Cole Randall tomorrow, I'm sure that will be soon enough."

"You want I should bring him in alive?"

"No—not necessarily."

"You want me to kill him for you?"

"I didn't say that."

"Say it, Mr. Harris."

"Really! This is all quite unnecessary! You're a strange man, Larn!"

"Say it, Harris."

Harris closed his eyes and took a deep breath. Then he opened his eyes and looked unflinchingly at Larn. "All right, Larn. I want you to kill him."

Larn smiled. "Yes, Mr. Harris. I *am* a strange man. But you're like everyone else, not strange at all. Greedy, perhaps. Ruthless—willing to do anything to get what you want, while you tell yourself how fine you are as you slip between your silk sheets at night. How much will you pay me if I bring him in dead, Mr. Harris?"

Harris had gone this far; he saw no reason to flinch now. "For yourself—two thousand."

"And for my men?"

"You'll have to split half that."

Larn nodded. "Agreed."

"Good day, Larn."

Larn did not bother to reply as Harris opened the door with a shaking hand and stepped out into the blazing, unreal sunlight. He felt as if he were fleeing some anteroom to hell after a conversation with the devil. Despite the sun's welcome heat, Harris shivered as he set off down the boardwalk, anxious to reach the cool, familiar sanctuary of his bank.

He was just passing The Lucky Lady when Judge Warner reeled out of the place and almost collided with him. The judge pirouetted away from Harris on unsteady legs. Then, aware it was Harris he was avoiding, he reeled back to the banker.

"Harris!" he cried, his small, red-rimmed eyes blazing fiercely. "What forces have you set in motion?" As he spoke, he almost lost his footing on the uneven boardwalk and reaching out with rheumatic hands clawed hold of Harris's wide lapels.

Cowpokes and townsmen passing the pair on their way in and out of The Lucky Lady looked on with amusement as Harris yanked the judge's hands from his lapel.

"We can't talk here, Judge!" Harris snapped.

"Where then?"

"My office," Harris replied, setting off quickly, eager to be away from the saloon entrance. "At the bank. Come along."

The judge pulled himself erect, brushed an imaginary speck of dust from his black frock coat, and started hustling after the banker. His effort to appear sober was a determined one and he was able to keep up with Harris without stumbling, despite the accursed uncertainties of the wooden sidewalk.

Harris waved the judge into the man's favorite stuffed armchair beside the banker's desk, then slumped into his swivel chair. He had told his clerk on entering his office with the judge that they were not to be disturbed. He leaned back in his chair now and peered with critical wariness at the already half-inebriated Judge William Warner. It was not yet two in the afternoon. The judge was getting an uncommonly early start this day, it seemed. The man blinked unhappily back at Harris as he tried to get his thoughts in order. He brightened suddenly and leaned forward.

"Say, Max, you wouldn't happen to have any of that imported hooch left, would you?"

Without a word Harris lifted his bottle of scotch and a glass from a desk drawer and poured a healthy dollop for the judge. He pushed the drink toward the judge and returned the bottle to the drawer and closed it.

Harris watched the man drink. Judge Warner was a failure at everything he had ever attempted. A florid Shakespearean actor who had come West to die dramatically of consumption, he had unaccountably thrown off the disease and so was turning to the bottle as an apt substitute. His sense of the dramatic, along with his encyclopedic knowledge of Shakespeare and other great poets, had given him a flair for sizing up situations, with the result that he soon found himself seated behind a bench, a gavel in his hand, dispensing justice of a theatrical, highly entertaining sort.

Since the man could be bought with marvelous ease, he had soon amassed a small fortune that Harris had recently tapped for his resurrection of the Northern & Central. The trouble now, it appeared, was that the judge was coming unstuck.

"What's wrong, Will?" Harris asked. "Isn't this somewhat early in the day for you to dive into your cups? Usually you're pretty coherent until after supper at least."

"My God, Max. Your hired gun has just brought in the bodies of two men! Since his arrival in this town, five men have died. Five men! You're sowing a wind, Max. Are you ready for the whirlwind—the inevitable whirlwind?"

"No," Harris replied dryly, "but I *am* ready for the railroad. Don't forget the railroad, Will. That'll make all this seem like a dose of castor oil to get rid of the ague—distasteful, but necessary."

"How much castor oil, Max?"

Harris took a deep breath. "Just a little, Will."

"How much?"

"Cole Randall."

The judge seemed quite sober all of a sudden, despite the fact that his glass was empty. He peered unhappily at Harris. "You're sending Danny Larn after him?"

Harris nodded.

"And most likely he'll bring him back the way he brought back Gunnison and Pete Anton."

Harris didn't think he needed to reply to that.

41

"Why not leave Cole Randall be, Max? You've already got his father. Now his ramrod and one of his hired hands."

"Hell, Will! Larn's got your warrant in his hands. It's all legal and proper. Don't forget that Cole Randall is capable of organizing the rest of the ranchers in that valley—or at least of sitrring up enough of a protest to put this thing in the courts. You know you can't afford that kind of a delay."

"We'd lose our shirts."

"Everything."

"We can't pull out?"

"I've already got two agents on the Continent signing up new settlers. This is lovely farm country, Will. Those dirty-necked foreigners are going to turn that valley into paradise and make us all rich in the bargain. In ten years you won't recognize this town. It won't be a town any longer, it'll be a city—a railhead. This is only the beginning, Will."

"Yes, Max. The beginning, all right. But the beginning of what?" He held out his glass. "How about a refill, Max—and you needn't be so careful this time."

Harris hauled out the bottle and filled the judge's glass. With a satisfied nod, the judge took up the glass and sipped the scotch.

"Did you know," he asked, "that Eliot Trace is demanding a grand jury be set up to investigate the circumstances surrounding Gunnison's and Anton's death? Doc Wilder, too, is furious. He's been telling anybody who'll listen that Pete Anton was shot in the back of his neck and that Gunnison was broken up pretty badly."

"They can set up all the grand juries they want, Will. Who's going to dispute what Danny Larn and his four deputies tell you? Hell, let them set up a grand jury. Maybe that'd be a good idea. Air the matter out and satisfy everyone. A neat whitewash."

Warner tossed down the rest of his scotch. The hooch

hit him like a gentle sledgehammer. "Perhaps," the man said. "Perhaps."

The bottle was still out on Harris's desk. "Here," he told the judge, holding out the bottle to him. "No sense in letting this go to waste."

"That's right," said the judge thickly. He closed his eyes for a full moment, then opened them wide and smiled with a sudden recklessness at Harris. "No sense in that. No sense at all."

As the judge took the bottle from Harris, Harris got to his feet and moved around from behind his desk. "You just stay right there, Judge," Harris told the man. "I've got some business to tend to out here."

"Go right ahead, Max. I've got my own business right in here."

Pausing at the door, Harris looked back at the cadaverous figure of Judge Warner. His hands like misshapen claws, his face like some gaunt bird of prey, the man nevertheless had a staying power that astonished Harris—a staying power and something else: for all his inebriation and all his theatrics, he had a way of seeing things with ominous clarity at times.

Harris left his office, feeling not half as confident as he had sounded when trying to calm the judge.

As he pulled the door shut, Harris beckoned to his clerk. The man hastened over.

"Judge Warner is resting up in my office. In about half an hour I want you to go in and help him across the street to his quarters. Is that clear?"

"Yes, Mr. Harris."

Harris nodded and strode from the bank. If the ranchers had their lawyer, he had his. Deal Wightman was a new man in town, but he was a shrewd one and had already been of invaluable assistance to the banker. Harris felt the need to consult with the man at once.

He hurried down the boardwalk, his massive, white-

maned head turned away from the bright, slanting rays of
the sun, his solid, hulking body moving at a considerable
pace.

Danny Larn stood at the back window of Pauline's and
looked out at the line of privies that squatted the length of
the back alley. He was in the nicest room in the place,
though it was still barely large enough to contain the bed.
The girl behind him on the bed stirred.

He turned quickly to face her. She watched him warily,
her large black eyes smoldering—not with lust, with fear.
She was new, all right. Too damn new. She hadn't been
able to do a thing for him!

"I ain't finished," he told her.

A passiveness fell over her face. She lay back down and
pulled the sheet up over her breasts and waited. Did he
detect the trace of a smile on her face? She better not be
laughing at him!

And then he realized she was looking at him. He looked
down at himself. Despair overwhelmed him. *Nothing!* With
a groan he threw himself onto the bed beside her. Swiftly,
her brown arm lifted the white sheet and let him snuggle
his pale body beside her duskiness.

Without a word she began to stroke his head. She seemed
to understand. He rested his cheek against her shoulder, the
bitterness within him dissolving slowly—to be replaced
with an enormous, aching emptiness.

The girl—her name was Maria—murmured softly as she
continued to stroke his head. He closed his eyes. . . .

*Danny heard his younger brother's screams while he
was still outside in the alley. He took the wooden stairs two
at a time, despite the short span of his ten-year-old limbs.
Bursting into the flat, he saw his father in the kitchen bent
over Billy. The little six-year-old was cowering on the floor,
his bony arms covering his head desperately as his father
flailed away at him with the buckle end of his belt.*

44

As Danny rushed through the kitchen doorway, he almost fell over the outstretched legs of his unconscious mother. She was lying on her back, her face already discoloring, one eye closed and bleeding. Danny had left her ironing to go to the store. His father had been gone for more than two weeks, on one of his frequent benders; he had returned during Danny's absence—and this was the result.

Danny took all this in during the moment it took him to cross the kitchen floor and fling himself at his father. The man grunting from the exertion of his labors and so intent on beating Billy that he had not seen Danny enter. Now he flung Danny back in sudden surprise. Danny caught the sickening whiff of whiskey and stale vomit as the man's forearm struck him. Danny was slammed back into the corner of the kitchen, his head striking the wall with numbing force.

His father went back to Billy, this time, it seemed, with renewed vigor. Billy, Danny saw, was no longer trying to protect his head. Danny became aware of the smell of burning cloth. He turned his head and saw the still hot iron resting on one of the shirts his mother had taken in to iron.

He snatched up the iron and scrambled to his feet. His father, still bent over Billy, was about to turn to deal with him. Danny brought the point of the iron down on the side of the man's head. His father said nothing. He simply slipped to one knee and lifted up one arm to ward Danny off. All Danny could think of then was that the man was not dead—that now he would really come after Danny and beat him as he had so often before. With a desperation born of despair he ran at his father and this time was able to bring the point of the iron down on the top of his father's head.

Danny felt the iron's tip lodge and then break through shattered bone. Dropping the iron, Danny watched as his father toppled soundlessly onto his side. A dark flower of blood bloomed from the broken skull, slicking the man's hair and puddling the bare wooden floor under his cheek.

45

He was wearing dirty woolens and a pair of stained trousers. As he died, he seemed to shrivel and pull himself into a ball, like any spider Danny might have struck from its web.

Billy was crying and holding on to his right ear. As Danny went to him, he heard his mother stir behind him. He turned to her just as she began to scream. She towered over him—both hands pressed to the sides of her head, her mouth open, her eyes wide and staring—and kept on screaming—a high, keening wail that cut through Danny like a knife.

Danny clapped both hands over his ears in an effort to blot out the shattering impact of her screams, but it did no good. He crawled into a corner and ducked his head, both ears covered. But there was nothing he could do to shut out his mother's screams. Nothing at all, ever. . . .

Danny moved convulsively. Maria stopped stroking him. He rolled out from under the sheet and sat up on the edge of the bed. He considered a moment, then reached for his boots.

"Get out," he told the girl. "Get out. I don't need you. I don't need anyone."

She was sitting up in the bed, her exposed breasts firm, the area around her nipples dark, like wide, wondering eyes.

"You heard me. Get out! I'll settle up with Pauline."

The girl threw back the sheet, snatched up her clothes, and darted from the room. Danny took a deep breath. He didn't care. It didn't matter. Despite the emptiness inside him, he could still function.

This thought comforted him enormously. Feeling much better, he reached for his creased trousers, folded neatly over the back of a chair. He would go after Cole Randall today. Hell, there was nothing at all wrong with the way he handled a gun.

Four

BILL GRAHAM finished his coffee with obvious relish, cleared his throat, and pushed his chair away from the table.

"I'm going out to check on those culls we just drove in from the breaks," he said to Linda and Cole. He smiled at Cole. "Have another cup of coffee, Cole, and visit with us." Winking at Linda, he said, "See if you can get this galoot to slow down some and rest a while."

"Oh, no," Linda said, laughing. "I'm going to ask him to help me with the dishes."

"I'm leavin'," said Bill, snatching his old hat from a peg by the door, "before I get roped in as well."

The old man strode out into the sunshine and left them.

Linda looked across the kitchen, a faint smile on her face. "Dad's not at all subtle, is he?"

"Never mind him," Cole said with a smile. "What about them dishes?"

She laughed. "Just take a minute. You give me a hand and maybe then we might have time for a short walk."

Cole realized that since he was on Box W land now, it gave Linda the courage to be more direct with him than she had been in a long time. He was almost in a mood to be amused by this sudden change in her. She had never really needed courage in her dealings with him or her father—or anyone else, for that matter.

It was just that lately, with her coming of age, it seemed, a subtle shift had occurred in the way she approached him— a shift that made her less open, less easy to be with, while at the same time everything she said to him and anything he said to her seemed to carry infinitely more weight than it used to. Everything that passed between them now seemed so blamed *delicate*. His sudden irritation at this, he realized too late, was undoubtedly reflected on his face. And Linda caught it at once.

"My!" she said with mock gravity. "If washing dishes makes you put on such a scowl, maybe we should just let them soak."

Cole laughed as easily as he could. "Good idea," he said. "Let's walk."

That pleased her. With one quick efficient movement she removed her apron, unconsciously straightened her long blue dress, and started ahead of him out the door. He followed her out, suddenly aware of the awesome importance of this little walk. Linda paused on the porch.

"Let's walk over there, by the alders," she said, pointing. "It's cool along the stream this time of day."

"Sure."

They walked across the compound together, saying little. He helped her through the corral fences, aware each time of how she hung back to let him lift her. Always before this, he could not help reflecting, she would be through or over the fences well before him, her small, lithe figure clothed in a cotton shirt and Levi's, her boots as worn and scuffed as her father's.

When they reached the alders, Linda dropped to the grass, her dress billowing prettily. She smoothed the skirt out and leaned her back against a tree and waited for Cole to sit down beside her. He did so awkwardly.

"I know I'm rushing things, Cole," she said.

He knew what she meant at once.

"You know what I mean, don't you, Cole."

He nodded.

"My," she said, "aren't we loquacious today."

"You *are* rushing things, Linda."

"But I have to know. I just can't . . ." She shrugged, reached down and snatched up a tuft of grass and began studying it intently.

"You can't wait, Linda?"

She looked at him then, boldly. "No, Cole Randall, I can't." She closed her eyes momentarily, as if astonished at her boldness—yet unable and unwilling to pull back now. "What I mean is now that you're going off like this—trying to get the rest of the ranchers to fight Harris and that awful Danny Larn—well, hang it, Cole, there's just too much *uncertainty*, that's all."

Cole grinned at her. "I guess you mean uncertainty about *us*, mostly. Isn't that it?"

She blushed scarlet. "Yes, smarty, that's right. About us. A girl has a right to know, especially when the fellow she's set her cap for is liable to get his fool head blown off if he's not careful."

He looked at her with sudden, immense affection. "Thanks, Linda. For caring, I mean. And for saying that you've set your cap for me. Any man would be right proud to have you set your cap for him."

"And you, Cole? What about you? Are *you* proud?"

"Of course, Linda."

"Oh, damn! What else could you say to a question like that! But that's not what I mean, anyway, Cole—and you know it."

"I guess I do, Linda."

"Well?"

He looked at her closely, seeing her for the first time—not as a hunting partner or as a friend he could take fishing when the ranch slowed down or for a ride when he wanted a companion during a long chase for strayed stock—but as a woman, *his* woman. Her finely sculpted fragility hid a steel core and the careless banter she had used all these years in communicating with him was her way of expressing the deep warmth and affection she had always felt for him. Even more than that, she was a brave and loyal friend who had never let him down.

Why then did he hesitate like this?

He frowned and looked away from her. "This ain't the time, Linda," he said. "Things are all going bad. Hell, I couldn't get one rancher besides your father to throw in with the Circle C. All I got left to ask is Wills of the Lazy S and Zeke Thomaris of the Flying O. Wills should throw in with us, but I'm not so sure about Thomaris. It just don't look so good, and I just can't seem to get my bearings."

"I see."

"You've been one hell of a fine friend all these years, Linda. You and your father. I'll never forget that. But I can't stand back and let the man who shot down my father get rich while he settles foreign nesters on Circle C land. I'm sorry, Linda, but I'm afraid that's the only thing in this world I *am* sure of."

"Of course, Cole. I understand."

He reached out and took her hand in his. She blushed. He found himself smiling at her again—and wondering how she would look with her tightly bound pigtails combed out so that her long dark lustrous hair tumbled down about her shoulders. She was really a very pretty girl, he realized. The thought encouraged him.

"Give me time, Linda. We both need it. But it's going to be all right. Just you wait and see. For both of us."

"You mean don't crowd you."

He took a deep breath. "I guess so, Linda. I guess that's what I mean."

"And that's . . . all you mean."

She was giving him an out. He took it. "Yes, Linda. For now . . . that's all I mean."

She smiled at him. It was a sunny smile that was so bright and blinding it successfully hid whatever she was thinking. "Fair enough," she said, getting to her feet. "Let's get back, Cole. I reckon you got some more hard riding to do, and I've still got that sink full of dishes waitin' for me."

"Hey, let me give you a hand with them."

"Wouldn't think of it," she said as she walked briskly along just out of his reach.

He knew from her tone that she meant it; and a moment later when they reached the corral fences, she was through well ahead of him with no hanging back this time to let him help her.

He said good-bye rather stiffly to her before they reached the ranchhouse, then went to the barn for his horse. A few moments later, as he rode through the gate he turned in his saddle and looked back. Linda was standing on the porch watching him ride out, as he knew she would be. He waved to her.

Linda watched until Cole was out of sight. Then she turned abruptly and hurried back into the kitchen, tears blinding her as she flung herself down at the table and buried her face in her arms. He hadn't said he loved her or that he wanted her. She had ached for him to take her in his arms, but he had never once moved toward her. She knew what she must be going through with the death of his father and had wanted to be able to comfort him, the way a woman comforts her man. But he had not let her.

She knew now—as clearly and as certainly as she had ever known anything in her life—that Cole Randall did not love her, that all these years she had waited in vain. . . .

Cole caught sight of Zeke Thomaris hazing a small gather up a slope behind his ranchhouse and waved to him. Zeke left his one hand to ride back down the slope and across the flat to his compound, arriving at the Flying O just ahead of Cole.

"Been expecting you, Cole," Zeke said, as he dismounted and walked across the yard toward Cole. "Light and rest a while."

As Cole swung out of his saddle, Thomaris called to his son, who had been standing in the barn doorway, a pitchfork in his hands, watching. "Take Cole's horse, Billy. Grain him and fill him a bucket of water from the spring."

"Yessir," the boy said, hurrying toward them from the barn.

When he reached up for the bridle to Cole's horse, his father mussed his twelve-year-old son's unruly shock of flaxen hair affectionately. "And take care of my cayuse too, will you, Billy?"

The boy grinned at his father. "Sure, dad. I would've anyway."

"Billy," said Cole, "keep my horse out of the shade if you can. He's been doing a lot of ridin' today."

The boy nodded quickly and led away the horses.

Cole looked at Zeke. "You say you were expecting me, Zeke?"

"Yep. I surely was. When I heard what happened to your pa, I figured you'd be looking for to get the cattlemen hereabouts together."

Cole nodded and the two men started for the ranchhouse.

Zeke's wife disappeared inside, obviously anxious to get a pot of coffee on the stove.

"I understand Gunnison was hit too."

"He was."

Thomaris shook his head. He was a tall, gangling individual with a long yellow handlebar mustache, deep-set eyes that peered out from under beetling brows, and a face as seamed and eroded as the poor, gullied high country over which he drove his cattle. "Terrible thing," the rancher said. "Just terrible. This man Harris has got to be stopped."

"Yes, he has."

The two men stepped into the cool, low-ceilinged interior of the ranch kitchen. The pot was singing softly on the stove and Zeke's wife was planting a sugar bowl and a heavy pitcher of cream down on the snowy linen tablecloth that now covered the deal table. The fold marks were still fresh in it, Cole noted.

"I was right sorry to hear about your father, Cole," Marie said, her pinched face serious with concern. "If there's anything I can do. . . ."

"Thanks, Marie. I do appreciate it. If there is anything you can do, I'll let you know. First thing."

That seemed to satisfy the woman, and she hastened back to the stove.

Zeke said, "It *was* the way I heard, wasn't it, Cole? I mean your father did go after Harris first."

"Yes, he did. And he fired first, too."

Zeke nodded unhappily, then leaned back to allow his wife to pour their coffee. "So what's your move now, Cole?"

"Like you figured. Organize the cattlemen. Hire a lawyer. Do what we can to tie Harris up in the courts."

Zeke looked craftily at Cole. "How's it goin', Cole? The rest of the ranchers stayin' with you?"

Cole looked at him without flinching. "Nope. The Box

W is all that's throwed in with me. And you're the last outfit on my list."

"I figured."

"Well?"

"Ain't usual for a valley outfit to go calling on a hill outfit like this one, Cole."

"I know that. But I need your help. I don't think I can stand up to Harris with just Bill Graham siding me. I don't think I can, but if I have to do it, I will."

"Well, you can count me on your side, Cole. But they ain't much of that valley land left for my beef to graze on when you fellers get through."

"How much do you think you'll have when Harris gets through emptyin' some village in Poland or Norway onto the valley?"

"What can I do, Cole?"

"Just help us pay for the lawyer and sign the complaint along with me and Bill Graham. You know what Don Willard told us when we settled here. All he wanted was the right of way, the rest of the land granted to his company he promised to sell at a reasonable price. But with Harris buying out Willard, we got us a horse of a different color. Harris is bound and determined to bring in settlers, and he wants all the land. That's why he's asking thirty dollars an acre. He knows damn well none of us are going to be able to come up with that."

"And if you do, he'll likely raise the ante."

"But that means we've got a case. Eliot Trace told my father last week that he would represent us if we wanted to go to court. At the time dad and I thought we could handle this without the courts." Cole shook his head bitterly and sipped the coffee. "I guess we were about as wrong as two men can be."

"Sure, Cole, I'll sign the complaint. But . . . how much cash are you going to need?"

Cole dropped his hand on Zeke's shoulder. "Don't worry

about that now, Zeke. I'll give you all the help you need on that score, no strings attached."

"Oh, I'm not poor-mouthin', Cole."

"I know that. But right now it's enough to know you're in my corner—not like those others I been talkin' to today." Cole shook his head in disappointment. He'd counted on more than the Flying O and the Box W to stand with him against Harris. Even Wills of the Lazy S had turned him down.

"If you're lookin' for another outfit to throw in with you, Cole, why don't you ride up to the Double Bar?"

Cole frowned. The Double Bar was a hard-scrabble outfit clinging to the side of Sawtooth Ridge, a couple of brothers and a hard-eyed sister running the outfit, as Cole recalled. He had seen the three of them in Broken Bow occasionally. Whenever they met Cole, they had regarded him, it seemed, with barely concealed hostility. Cole had heard them called the Doblers.

"They're out of this, aren't they, Zeke?"

"Mebbe, mebbe not." He looked closely at Cole. "They been usin' the northern portion of the valley for some of their new stock."

"They have?"

"That's right, Cole."

Cole nodded thoughtfully. By rights that was Circle C land. It always had been, at any rate. That high pasture was always good late in the summer when the flats got over-grazed or burnt off. Cole looked at Zeke with a thin smile. "I guess they figure Circle C's got plenty of land to spare."

"'I've heard them say that, Cole."

Cole nodded. This explained their attitude whenever their trails crossed. Aware they were grazing Circle C pasture, they were primed for trouble. "Funny Mike didn't catch wise."

"They always pulled their stock out of the valley before Mike sent any beef onto it. Then there was a couple summers there where the rain kept the valley lush enough so's you didn't need to move your cattle."

"You know all about it, Zeke."

"Yep. They been good neighbors, Cole. A hard-working outfit."

"But not very honest."

"They only eat their own beef, Cole, and they been keeping out of your way. If they've been stretchin' it some usin' that part of the valley, it ain't hurt you none, has it?"

Cole considered a moment. Of course, it hadn't. But that wasn't the point. Marie poured fresh coffee into his cup. She was listening to every word, and Cole could tell she was concerned that what Zeke had disclosed would anger Cole. As Cole thanked her for the coffee and spooned sugar into it, he considered what his father's reaction would have been.

The man's immediate reaction would have been fury. He would have saddled up at once and, with his riders at his back, he would have ridden onto the Double Bar ranch with a Winchester across his pommel, fire in his eyes, and a measured threat in his words. It would have been as simple and as direct as that. To allow any flea-bitten outfit like the Double Bar to feed off any portion of their grass would doom the outfit in his eyes. It would encourage every nickel-and-dime outfit in the territory to move in and nibble Circle C to death.

At last Cole met Zeke's eyes. "It's a precedent, Zeke. That's the problem."

Zeke nodded. "For you it's precedent. For them, survival."

Cole took a deep breath and smiled wearily at Zeke. "It's survival for Circle C now, isn't it." He glanced across the kitchen at Marie. "Times like this an outfit needs all the help it can get." Marie brightened in relief. Cole looked back at Zeke. "You think the Double Bar might be interested in throwing in with Circle C on this?"

Zeke leaned back in his chair, relieved. "Sure. Why not, since they're just as concerned as you are about losing that valley land to settlers."

Cole nodded thoughtfully. "Sure enough. You might almost say we're partners already."

"You might at that," said Zeke with a grin.

Cole pushed himself to his feet. "Then I guess I'll be going, Zeke. Thanks for the hospitality, Marie," he said to the woman.

"You just take care of yourself, hear?" she called after him as he strode toward the door.

Snugging down his hat, Cole glanced back at her. "I'll do that, Marie, best as I can."

Zeke stood with him on the low porch. "Billy!" he called. "Bring Cole's mount! He's ridin' up to the Double Bar!"

Billy ran from the barn. "His bay's pretty done in, pa!"

Zeke looked at Cole. "Take that roan of mine, Cole. No sense in riding your hoss to death. You got tough country to travel before you reach the Double Bar."

"Much obliged, Zeke."

"Billy," Zeke said, "put Cole's horse out to pasture. He'll be stayin' with us a while. And bring Cole the roan."

Billy turned and vanished back into the shadows of the barn.

Three hours later, higher by at least a couple of thousand feet, Cole rode out of timber and found himself on Razorback Ridge. He followed the rutted trail through the great humped boulders and dropped down a gentle slope beyond to a lower shelf. Some cattle with the Double Bar brand stood somnolently on the table, watching him vaguely. They were lean, Cole thought, but a long way from starving out.

The trail led across the tableland to a dark stand of timber on the horizon. He was within a hundred yards of the woodland when he caught the glint of sunlight on a gun barrel, like cat's eyes in the night. He ducked low over his mount's neck and put his spurs to him, running for a knoll to his right, behind which the treeline coiled.

The rifle shot came an instant later and Cole heard the whisper of the round's passage just above his head. He bent still lower over his horse's neck as the second round hummed past. He was shooting high, Cole realized. From the sound of the bullet and of the rifle's crack, he knew the man was firing a Winchester .44/40.

And then he was swinging off his mount, pulling his own Winchester from its sling as he did so. The knoll was just high enough to give both him and the roan cover. On his knees and elbows he snaked to the crest of the knoll and peered over. So far, all he had seen was that giveaway glint of light on gunmetal.

He watched silently, not moving an inch, for close to five minutes while his eyes slowly grew accustomed to the dimness within the trees and became able to pick out more details—a bush here, the face of a boulder there, a stunted pine, a birch that had cracked through a rock. His eyes narrowed suddenly and he glanced back at the birch.

Yes, there it was—the barely visible crown of a hat.

Aiming with infinite care, he squeezed off a shot. The round whined as it slanted off the rock. The hat vanished. He smiled and levered another cartridge into the firing chamber. The next round he put lower, into the trunk of a tree flanking the birch and just a bit behind it. He saw quick movement and then stillness just behind the birch. Cole had whoever it was pinned nicely.

He snaked back down the knoll swiftly and bent over nearly double, raced across the short stretch of grassland to the line of trees, keeping the knoll between him and the bushwacker. Once in the trees, he circled back down the slope and then worked his way through the timber toward the open flat. He came upon the fellow's horse—a big fat grulla wearing the Double Bar brand—tethered in a small clearing. Crouching low, he skirted the horse, anxious not to cause him to whicker.

The birch appeared through the trees just ahead of him. Stepping cautiously, he parted some bushes blocking him and caught sight of a long-legged fellow prone behind the cracked rock. His Winchester was beside him in the grass, and to Cole's surprise the fellow was nursing a slight flesh wound high on his arm. That second bullet must have ricocheted off the tree he had been aiming for—a lucky shot. The fellow was hanging on to a bandanna he had stuck into the sleeve of his sheepskin jacket to stem the flow of blood. His large black, flop-brimmed hat hid his face, with the collar of his jacket well up around his neck. Cole stepped through the bushes, careless of any sound he made.

"Freeze right there," he said. "Don't move a goddamned muscle or I'll blow a hole through your backside."

Cole grinned as he saw the cheeks of the fellow's ass tense as the rest of his body froze. He stepped close to him and reached down and took the rifle. Flinging it to one side into the brush, he poked the boot of his right toe under the fellow's thigh and kicked him over onto his back.

He found himself looking into the dark, furious eyes of a young woman. Her thick chestnut curls had been drawn in under her chin and spilled down now over her faded blue men's shirt pulled tight across her bosom. She had opened her jacket to get more comfortable presumably and Cole saw that gaps threatened to open between the two top button sets of the shirt.

She sure as hell looked some different from the front.

"Damn you!" she said, seething. "Where in hell'd you come from?"

Cole stepped back. He was startled, but not so badly that he forgot that this Dobler girl had just tried to kill him.

"What's the idea, ma'am? You in the habit of bushwhacking people—or did you mistake me for an Indian?"

"An Indian I wouldn't have shot at—Cole Randall is a different matter," she snapped icily.

"Ma'am, you do talk spitefully, at that. What in hell did I ever do to you or Double Bar to warrant all this spittin' and cussin'?"

She looked away, suddenly guilty, and reached for her wound. "I'm wounded," she said angrily. "You caught me in the arm."

"I usually do hit what I aim at, ma'am. It's a habit of mine."

"I wasn't aimin' to hit you, damn it. If I had, you'd still be out there on that flat now."

"Then why?"

"To warn you off. You're on Double Bar land!"

Cole sighed and took a step back, leaning his rifle against a tree. "Can you get up?"

"Yes," she said, coiling first to her knees, then getting to her feet. She held the bandanna to her arm all the while.

"You better take that jacket off and let me have a look at that wound."

She looked at him for a moment, pure venom in her eyes. "I'll be all right," she said, "as soon as I get back to the ranch."

"Good. I'll ride with you. I was coming up to see you and your brothers anyway. But I haven't met any of you formally, so this way you can introduce me." He tried a smile, but she did not return it.

"Why?" Her eyes narrowed with suspicion. He knew she was thinking of what Zeke had told him.

"It's not about you using the north valley."

She was startled.

"You knew about that?"

He nodded.

"For how long?"

"That's not important, is it?"

She was uncertain now as to how to regard him. "I guess not. So why were you nosin' around?"

"I told you. I was coming up to see you and your brothers."

"I'm still asking why."

"This trouble with the railroad—Banker Harris, to be specific. Since your spread and mine are using the valley to our mutual advantage, I figured you might want to join the rest of us cattlemen who are trying to stand up to Harris."

"We might, but I ain't going to speak for my brothers."

"That's why I would like you to take me to them, introduce me to them." Cole smiled. "I might have a tough time, otherwise, seeing as how I shot their sister." Again, his smile was not returned.

She pulled the bandanna out of the hole in her sheepskin's sleeve and looked at the wound. She moved her arm quickly. "It's only a flesh wound, and it's already stopped bleeding, though the lining of this jacket's probably ruined. My hoss is back there. But where in blazes did you toss my rifle?"

"Get your mount. I'll get your rifle and go for my horse. We can meet out on the flat."

She nodded curtly and started back through the timber for her horse. He watched her for a moment, impressed by the way she filled out her Levi's. Come bedtime, it looked like she'd have to peel them off.

For the next hour that they rode over the high, boulder-strewn country, Cole got little more out of her than her first name and that of her two brothers. She was Nancy, her brothers were Blue and Ryan. Her wound seemed not to trouble to her in the least, now that it was no longer bleeding—and he could not help remarking to himself what a fine rider she was. She rode easily, relaxed in the saddle, leaning her weight lazily into the stirrups.

He was still trying to generate some conversation, without much success, when the trail curled around a thin stand of cedar, climbed a short slope, and came into view of the clustered buildings of a ranch, a low jumble of weathered dark shapes at the far end of a grassy table. The ranchhouse and its outbuildings took on detail swiftly as they drew closer.

A small stream trickled along the south side of the flat at the base of timbered hills. It meandered across the flat at one point, and Cole forded it with Nancy leading the way. The stream was shallow, hardly more than a trickle. Spring-fed, Cole guessed, and a trickle like that would quickly run aground, but it explained the lush green of the meadow. Indeed, much of this high country was alive with spring-fed streams, which meant that this outfit need not be as hard-scrabble and desperate as one might have thought. Still, that portion of the high valley they were using in the early months of summer would still be needed to give their calves a good start after winter.

As he rode into the yard alongside Nancy, a tall fellow came out of the ranchhouse door and stood on the porch, one hand on a post, a frown on his lean face. "Look what the cat drug in," he drawled.

Another fellow—shorter, huskier—stepped through the open doorway behind him and took his place beside his brother. His face was sullen, resentful. Obviously he recognized Cole.

"Never mind that, Blue," said Nancy, addressing the taller brother. "He knows about our using Circle C land."

Blue pushed himself away from the porch post and chucked his hat back off his forehead, his steel-blue eyes regarding Cole coldly. "Hell, it was only a matter of time before he found out. We always knew that."

As Nancy dismounted, favoring her left arm, the smaller brother stepped forward, his eyes narrowing with sudden concern. "Hey, sis! You been shot?"

"A flesh wound, that's all."

Both brothers had their guns out and trained on Cole in

the instant it took for her to reply. Cole sat his horse quietly and smiled at them. "Ain't you going to ask me to light, boys? You're acting plumb inhospitable."

"Put those six-guns away," said Nancy, starting up the porch steps. "I drew down on him first. He didn't know who it was shooting at him. And like I said, it's just a flesh wound."

The two men hesitated a moment, then holstered their guns. Nancy, standing beside her brothers, turned to face Cole, her face unsmiling and hard.

"Light, Randall, and come inside. Even though I'm all wounded to hell, I'll fix us some coffee. Then you can tell us why you came up here. And what you want."

As Cole dismounted, the three of them turned their backs on him and went ahead of him into the ranchhouse. When Cole entered the ranchhouse, he found himself in a long narrow room, dominated by a huge stone fireplace along one wall. There were hunting trophies above the long mantelpiece—a buck with an impressive spread of antlers, an elk, and a moose. Comfortable leather chairs were spotted about the room and one long leather sofa. The rough board floor was covered for the most part by two bear rugs. It was a man's place, Cole thought, wondering at the lack of any sign of a woman's touch—of any indication at all that one of the three occupants of this ranch was a woman.

Nancy and her brothers led Cole into the kitchen, a smaller room off the main room. A great black wood stove sat in a corner, a wide deal table dominating the kitchen. Solid homemade wood chairs surrounded the table. Cole picked one and sat down, tipping his hat wearily back off his forehead. He became suddenly aware of how much traveling he had done during this day—and what had happened to him these last three. He was more than weary; he was exhausted, but a glance around him at the three tense faces told him that he was not going to be able to relax just yet.

As Nancy moved over to the stove, the two brothers

pulled out chairs and sat down facing him. It was the tall one, Blue, who spoke first.

"All right. Let's have it. You comin' after us just because we sneaked some cattle onto your land?"

Cole shook his head wearily. "No."

"Then what're you doin' way up here? You big cattle men don't usually have much truck with hard-scrabble outfits like this one. We're beneath your notice."

"Usually."

The chunkier brother spoke up then. "I don't think it's got anything to do with that valley pasture, Blue. I just rode in and ain't yet had a chance to tell you what's been happening."

"Well," snapped Blue impatiently, "let's have it. What's been happening?"

Ryan leaned back, obviously savoring the moment. "You won't believe this."

"For heaven's sake, Ryan," complained an exasperated Nancy from the stove, "can't you ever tell anything straight?"

Ryan flinched at the scorn in his sister's voice. "Randall's pa—and a couple of his hands," he said. "Harris shot his pa and Danny Larn just brought in the Circle C ramrod and one of his riders this morning—dead as doornails, by hell."

"What did you say?" Cole asked, rising out of his seat. "What was that about my ramrod and one of his riders?"

"You heard me," Ryan said, looking up at Cole with a sudden frown on his face. "I thought you'd heard by now."

"About my father, yes. I buried him yesterday. But my ramrod took a buckboard into Broken Bow this morning. I rode with him part way. He was all right then. He needed some attention from the doctor, that's all. One of my hands was driving the buckboard. Like I said, they were both all right when I left them. Damn your eyes, man! You got your facts straight here?"

"Well, they weren't all right this morning when they

finally got to Broken Bow—slung over the back of a horse."

Cole took a deep breath. It was what he had feared. If only he had ridden further with them—into town, in fact. "You said Danny Larn brought them in."

"That's what I said. I was standing across the street from Stitch Anderson's barber shop when Larn and his deputies pulled up in front of it with the bodies."

Cole's mouth went dry. The anger he felt made him weak on his feet.

"Sit down, Randall," said Blue, his face no longer a hard mask, his eyes revealing a spark of sympathy.

Nancy hurried over with a heavy crockery mug of steaming coffee and placed it down in front of Cole. "I'll get the whiskey to go with that," she said to Blue as she turned to a cupboard over the sink.

Slowly Cole sank back into his chair.

"I . . . thought you knew," said Ryan. "I thought that was why you was here."

Cole looked at him carefully. "What do you mean?"

"You need a place to hide. Larn's got a warrant for your arrest too, I hear."

"That's not why I rode up here." Cole let Nancy pour a generous portion of the whiskey into his coffee. "I figured, since we're partners in a sense—both using the valley land—you might want to join me in trying to block Harris from pushing the railroad through the valley and dumping a trainload of settlers on the land."

"Partners, you say?" Blue asked, tipping his head slightly. "What the hell you mean by that?"

"I told you what I meant. You need that valley land, don't you?"

"Sure. But I don't remember any talk between us about forming a partnership."

Nancy broke in then as she set down mugs of coffee before her brothers. "He's tryin' to say that he don't mind us usin' the land, and that he needs our help, Blue. Don't make it so hard for him."

Ryan looked up at her in astonishment. "And you carryin' a wound he inflicted on you? You gettin' soft, sis?"

"You heard him, Ryan. Where's your manners? You turning into some kind of an animal? He just told us he buried his father yesterday—and now he's lost his ramrod. Is all you can see in that some kind of an advantage?" She sat down next to her brother and looked at Cole. "How do you plan on stopping Harris?" she asked. "He owns the right of way, don't he?"

"And large government grants on both sides of the right of way," Cole said, "but if we can get enough cattlemen in this area to get together, maybe my lawyer can get an injunction, slow Harris down some. We settled this land under the assumption we would be able to buy that granted land from the railroad at reasonable prices. We didn't sign any papers, but that was the agreement."

"But that won't stop Harris for long, will it?" Blue asked.

"Once we get it into the courts, we can delay him long enough to make it impossible for him to finance it. It's those settlers he's countin' on to give him back his investment—and those of his other backers."

"If you stop Harris, you'll stop the railroad from coming in. Hell, Randall, this country could use a railroad."

"This high country won't need a railroad for shipping its cattle if Harris has his way. There won't be that much land left for prime graze."

"Maybe not down there on those lovely flats. But we'll get by up here just fine."

"Anything that hurts cattle raising in this country hurts it for all of us."

"He's right," said Nancy. "We've got to stick together in this, or we'll all go down the drain."

Blue nodded and leaned back in his chair, his steady eyes regarding Cole with little warmth. "We been pounding our asses riding this high, rimrock country without no help from you big boys in the basin. We wasn't good enough to wipe your sweat. Never called us in once during a roundup. The only time you ever went lookin' for us was when you misplaced some beef and came looking for it in our herds, without so much as a by your leave, mister—and now you want us to work with you. Now, all of a sudden-like, we're grand partners. Is that it?"

"That's it," said Cole dryly.

"Hell, I don't know, Randall. I just don't know. If a guy's on his way to hell on a runaway broomtail, ain't no sense in hitching a ride with him. Not that I can see, mister."

Cole decided not to respond to that. Instead he sipped the still-hot whiskey-laced coffee and waited for them to answer that question themselves. He was in no mood to argue the point. With each passing second his mood blackened. The coffee did not help. He understood perfectly how they felt. Everything Blue had just told him was true. But if they could not see how this business affected them—just as so many other of his fellow ranchers could not see it—then he would accept their decision without comment, and get on with seeing to Maxwell Harris and that mad dog he had loosed upon Circle C.

"Who else's throwin' in with you, Randall?" Ryan asked.

"The Box W and the Flying O."

"The Flying O?" Nancy said, her brows raising. "That's Zeke Thomaris's outfit, ain't it?"

Cole nodded.

Nancy looked at Blue. "They've always played square with us. Always."

"I know that," admitted Blue. "Never said they didn't. So what's that prove?"

"Damnit, boys! You afraid of tangling with that money-lender and his hired gun?"

Ryan stirred uneasily under his sister's angry gaze. "You know that ain't true, sis."

"I hate the son-of-a-bitch, and that's a fact," said Blue, smiling thinly.

Nancy turned to Cole. "When we first reached this territory about three years ago, we went to Harris for a loan. He laughed at us. Called us mountain trash—said he knew the type. Wouldn't lend us a copper."

Ryan said, "We ain't got no love for the man. Sure enough. But that don't mean we got to throw in with you. That Danny Larn is death in a hurry, if I ever saw it."

"But we're not afraid of either," said Blue quietly.

"No," said Ryan. "We ain't."

Nancy didn't exactly smile, but her eyes softened as she looked at Cole and extended her hand. "Count us in," she said.

Cole took the hand of the girl and was impressed with its strength. And then he shook hands with the two men, feeling better at once.

"It's late. Dusk comes fast up here," Nancy said, getting to her feet and clearing off the table. "You'd better not try to ride back down this late. You better stay the night. You're welcome."

Cole glanced out the window. Nancy was right. Dusk was falling. Already Cole felt the cool chill in the air. "I'm much obliged, Nancy."

"You can get a fresh start in the morning," Blue said, nodding his approval of Nancy's suggestion.

"All of us," said Nancy.

"No, not all of us," said Blue. "Someone's got to stay here to watch things. Ryan and I will ride in with Cole. I'm anxious to get a look at this Danny Larn I been hearin' so much about."

"We'll argue about who goes tomorrow morning," Nancy said quietly but firmly. "Now you three get out of here so's I can rustle up some supper."

Cole left the kitchen with the two men and strode out onto the porch. The moment Nancy had extended her hand to him, the tension in the room had broken. The Doblers were throwing in with him at a time when they knew just how cruel and uncompromising the odds were—and Cole had the feeling they would hang tough, come what may.

"Come on," said Blue, turning to Cole with a faint smile on his lean face. "We'll show you around some. Take your mind off things."

Cole nodded and left the porch with the two men, grateful for the diversion—though nothing, he knew, could quell the sad, choking rage that had built within him the moment he had learned of Pete's and Mike Gunnison's deaths.

Five

ZEKE THOMARIS pulled up smartly and stepped to the door of his small blacksmith shed, the smoking tongs still held in his right hand. He had been reaching for the bellows when he caught the movement atop the south ridge.

Now he stood perfectly still, his yellowed handlebar mustache drooping ominously around his mouth, his eyes narrowed in concentration beneath his bushy brows. Five riders. Coming in a hurry, judging from the dust they were raising. He waited a while longer until he made out the lead rider.

He was dressed in a dark coat, dark trousers, a light Stetson, and an immaculate white bandanna at his throat. The sun brightened it as he rode. Danny Larn and his so-called deputies, come to fetch Cole Randall.

"What is it, pa?"

Billy had been hauling water for the forge tank and was standing now just behind Zeke with an empty bucket in his hand. He had not yet seen the riders. Zeke stepped out of the doorway and turned to Billy.

"Go out this back door, Billy, and high-tail it to the barn. You hear?"

Billy nodded and quickly put down the bucket.

"And don't come back to the ranchhouse no matter what happens and no matter what you see. Am I gettin' through to you, boy?"

"Yes, pa!" The urgency in his father's voice was beginning to frighten Billy.

Zeke's face softened. He reached out and took the boy by the arms and held him steady. "No need to get frightened, Billy, if you do like I say."

The boy nodded dutifully.

"You keep your ears open. If the riders are looking for Cole Randall, you wait your chance and sneak out the back of the barn and ride to the Double Bar and warn Cole. I'll try to keep these men here as long as I can. Use Cole's horse and ride him without a saddle. He's in the lower forty somewhere. Can you do that, Billy?"

"Sure, pa."

Zeke nodded briskly, then slapped Billy lightly on the rump. "Then go!"

The boy was through the back of the shed in a twinkling and crossed the open ground between the blacksmith shed and the barn on the dead run. With the shed between Billy and the oncoming riders, Zeke was certain they had not seen his boy.

Zeke was anxious that Cole be warned; but his foremost concern was the safety of his boy—and Marie. He knew from experience what darkness lived in the hearts of these killers on horseback and sensed instinctively how they would use the boy or Marie to gain their ends.

Zeke hurried across the yard into the ranchhouse. Marie was kneading some bread dough on the deal table. She looked up in surprise as he entered.

"Finished that wagon wheel already!" she asked.

"Riders coming. They'll be here right soon at the rate they're moving. I figure it's that Danny Larn and his gunslicks looking for Cole. I sent the boy to hide in the barn. I want you to make yourself scarce."

Marie stepped back from the table and brushed the palms of her hands down the front of her apron, her face as pale as the flour she left on the apron. Zeke noticed then how fragile his wife appeared. At moments like this he chided himself for his unthinking selfishness in bringing this dolllike woman out to such a grim and lonely place. The worst of it was she never complained. Never. But he saw daily how unrelentingly hard it was for her. And now this.

"Go into the bedroom." he told her, walking over to the wall over the fireplace and reaching down his Winchester. "Stay in there. I'll handle this outside. I won't let them in."

She nodded without a word. As she closed the bedroom door behind her, Zeke stepped out onto the low porch and pulled the door shut behind him. There was a chill in the air as the sun got ready to dip below the horizon. The setting sun was striking the oncoming riders full on, giving all their faces a singularly livid cast.

They rode full-tilt through the gate and clattered to a halt in front of the ranchhouse. Zeke levered a fresh cartridge into the Westchester's firing chamber.

Danny Larn smiled at Zeke while he settled down his horse with a negligent pat on the side of the animal's neck. "Been ridin' hard," Larn said.

Zeke did not respond.

"After a skunk."

"That so?"

"You'd be Zeke Thomaris, wouldn't you."

"That's right."

"Been trailing Cole Randall. Got a warrant for his arrest, for the murder of U.S. Marshal Poole."

Zeke shifted the rifle in his hands.

"His trail leads to your place. Those other ranchers he tried to get to throw in with him were plumb anxious to cooperate. Frank Wills of the Lazy S said he was heading here, last he heard. That's what Randall told him anyways."

"He was here, all right."

Larn smiled thinly. "We know that."

"He's gone now."

"We know that, too. Where'd he go, Thomaris?"

"Back to town."

"You're a liar, Thomaris. We just came that way. We'd have crossed his trail if he was headin' that way." Larn leaned forward over the cantle. "Did you throw in with him, Thomaris?"

"That ain't none of your business."

"You did, then."

Zeke said nothing.

"Where'd he go, Thomaris?"

"Back to his spread, maybe. How should I know? He left here pretty discouraged."

"You threw in with him, so he would have told you his plans. You know which way he went."

"All right. He went back to his spread."

"No, he didn't, Thomaris."

"How the hell do you know?"

Larn smiled. "Just tell us which direction he took, Thomaris. We know he didn't ride south. And hurry it up. It'll soon be too dark for us to track him. Besides, we're saddlesore."

"I told you. I don't know where he went after he left here."

Larn studied Zeke for a long moment. As he did, the riders backing Larn smiled and urged their mounts closer.

They reminded Zeke of a ring of wolves contemplating a lame deer they were about to pull down. Each rider's eyes narrowed in anticipation as Larn considered his next move.

Abruptly Larn sighed and turned to a rider who had pulled close to him, and shrugged—as if to say it was out of his hands now. The fellow—a long-legged, bony fellow with eyes set deep in dark hollows—nodded and swung out of his saddle.

"See if you can jog his memory," Larn said to him.

Miles smiled, then coughed abruptly, his bony shoulders heaving convulsively. He straightened after the spasm and waved two men out of their saddles. They dismounted eagerly and started toward the porch.

Zeke pointed the rifle at Larn. "Call off your dogs, Larn, or I'll blow you off that horse."

The two men paused and glanced up at Larn. Larn leaned back in his saddle and regarded Zeke with amusement. "By the time you lift that rifle to your shoulder, Thomaris, you'll be dead."

As he spoke, his gleaming six-gun appeared—as if by some incredible slight-of-hand—in his right fist. The muzzle was aimed at Zeke's belly.

Zeke was dismayed by the suddenness of it—the incredible ease. He felt the palms of his hands begin to sweat. "I'm warning you," he said, his voice betraying his uncertainty.

"Sure. You're warning me. And I'm telling you. You might knock me on my ass before I can pull this trigger. But then again, you might miss. And you know damn well I won't." Larn smiled, a cold, mirthless smile. "I'm a gunman. Killing is my business. You're just an overaged cowpoke with more land than sense. Think it over."

Zeke thought it over. Larn's insolent honesty made a powerful point. The man was right: he was no match for a professional killer, especially for this one who came riding in behind a badge. Slowly, Zeke lowered his rifle.

At once the two men strode quickly forward and mounted the porch. One of them took the rifle from him and flung it into the yard. The other grabbed Zeke from behind, pinning his arms. The fellow who had flung away the rifle turned to Zeke and buried his right fist deep into Zeke's gut. Zeke felt the blow as a driving wedge of pain that exploded deep within him. He gagged and tried to double over, but he was held firmly upright as the fellow punched him a second time. As the pain swarmed up his backbone and exploded in his skull, Zeke thought he was going to throw up. He tried to bend over, but still the powerful arms held him from behind. A third time the fist was rammed into his gut, this time with such force that Zeke was certain the man had cracked his spine. He gagged convulsively. The hands holding him from behind released him and he pitched forward off the porch and landed in the midst of his own vomit. Twisting convulsively away, he felt brutal hands lifting him to his feet again.

Through red-glazed eyes he saw the man Larn called Miles peering at him intently. Zeke tried to spit in the fellow's face. The man stepped back quickly, then ducked his head and began coughing violently. This time he reached for a filthy bandanna and held it to his mouth. As he continued to hack into the cloth, he nodded to the other two.

The fellow went for Zeke's head this time, for which Zeke was dimly grateful. After trying futilely to pull away, he let it happen and soon felt himself almost floating to the ground. He didn't remember striking it, but he did remember the sudden bludgeoning of the bucketful of water that was thrown on his face to revive him.

They began to kick him then, panting furiously, carried away by their enthusiasm. Zeke pulled himself into a ball, his knees drawn up, his arms covering his ears. Again he sank into a blessed unconsciousness and again a bucket of water was brought and dumped on him. Someone hauled him upright.

Again Miles stepped closer. "How about it, Thomaris? Where did Randall go?"

"Up . . . your . . . ass, mister . . ."

Larn stepped back and signaled to the two men.

"Stop it! Stop it, I say! You get away from him!"

Through the fog of pain Zeke recognized Marie's voice. He twisted his head and made out the small figure of Marie standing in the open doorway of the ranchhouse, an enormous old army Colt held in both her hands. The muzzle wavered as the weight of the old cap-and-ball pistol pulled her hands down.

"No, Marie!" Zeke murmured through broken, puffed lips. "Put it down, Marie! Put it down!"

The two men who had been about to yank him to his feet and set to work on him again took a step back from Zeke and laughed. Zeke heard Larn's quiet chuckle as well. And then the man spoke, almost gently.

"Put down that horse pistol, ma'am. It's liable to go off and hurt someone—most likely you."

"You leave him be!" she cried, tears of rage coursing down her cheeks. "You leave him be!"

"Why, sure, ma'am. No reason to beat the poor fellow any longer. He obviously ain't going to tell us whichaway Cole went." Zeke heard Larn's saddle squeak as the man shifted his position. "Stand back, boys! Leave that stubborn old fool alone."

Zeke blinked up blearily at the two men as they stepped well away from the porch, then turned. Zeke rolled over onto his stomach, gathered all his strength and pulled his knees up under his body, gritting his teeth against the pain, then heaved himself to his feet. He reached out and just managed to grab hold of one of the porch posts. Clinging to this, he turned to face Larn and his tormentors.

"Get out of here now," he rasped. "Mount up and get off my land!"

Larn said, "You tell that woman of yours to put down

that pistol. Or I just might try shooting it out of her hand."
The man still held his bright Smith & Wesson.

"Marie," Zeke said to her, "put it down. Please."

Slowly, Marie lowered the Colt.

Larn nodded swiftly to Miles. The man sprang to the
porch and wrested the Colt from Marie's hand. As Zeke let
go of the post and attempted to stop Miles, the fellow
brought the gun up in a vicious arc, caught Zeke under the
chin, and sent him hurtling back against the log wall of the
ranchhouse. Dazed, knocked almost insensible by the force
of the blow, he felt himself slipping slowly down the wall.
The right side of his face seemed inordinately numb and
his right eye seemed unable to focus as a red film grew over
it.

Zeke heard Marie scream. She had been hurrying to his
side when the two men who had worked him over grabbed
her from behind and flung her roughly against the porch
post. As she struggled to free herself from their grasp, one
of the men slapped her smartly. Zeke saw this and groaned.

"Now listen to me, Thomaris!" Larn called to him. "And
listen good!"

Zeke tried to struggle upright to gain Marie's side. Miles
mounted the porch and planted a kick in Zeke's side, just
under his ribs. Zeke groaned and fell back.

"I said listen!"

Zeke lay still, his mouth open as he gulped in air, his
head tipped so that he could see Larn with his good left
eye.

"That's better. Now you tell us whichaway Cole Randall
went or we'll start on your little wife here. That slap was
just the beginning. You think Cole Randall's worth all that,
why you just keep on lyin' to us."

Zeke panted a moment, then held up his hand, palm out,
to hold them off. Larn smiled and leaned close.

"Speak up, man!"

"He went to the Double Bar . . . to ask them to throw in with him."

Larn sat back in his saddle and looked long at Zeke, then nodded abruptly. "Sounds logical. He sure wasn't striking fire with them other ranchers. He wouldn't want to go back to the Circle C empty-handed. You figure that outfit might throw in with him?"

"I told him . . . it might."

"Now where is this outfit?"

Zeke moved his head slightly. "North . . . beyond Razorback Ridge."

"How far would you say?"

"Three-, four-hour ride."

Larn swung off his horse. "We'll rest up a while here then while you give us some better directions than that."

With his gun in hand, he indicated they should precede him into the ranchhouse. Zeke struggled to his feet, Marie helping him. Then, with her arm still about him, Zeke moved into his ranchhouse, the crowd of men moving in after him.

Billy stumbled repeatedly as he raced over the darkening flat, the bridle and reins clutched in one hand, a full canteen in the other. It was tears, distorting his vision, as well as the dusk that made it so difficult to run smoothly over the uneven ground.

He kept seeing in his mind's eye his father going down again and again under the cruel, bludgeoning blows of that man. And then his mother . . . ! A sob broke from him as he went tumbling forward over a low boulder. Just ahead of him was Cole's bay. It nickered nervously and pulled back, its ears flattening, as Billy fell. Billy fought back the sobs and sat up. He took a couple of deep breaths, then got slowly to his feet and started toward the bay. The bay whisked its tail nervously and swung around to face him, ears flicking. Billy kept moving toward him, speaking softly, gently. Abruptly, the bay swung his head around and took off down a gentle rise at an easy canter. Despair momentarily flooded Billy.

But he forced himself to calm down, then started at a light trot after the horse. When he got to within ten yards of the bay, Billy sat down on a boulder and began fingering the bridle. After a while the bay looked up at him curiously, its ears reaching forward. Billy ignored the horse. With a curious nicker, the bay trotted suddenly over to Billy and pushed at Billy's shoulder with a moist nose.

Billy reached up quickly, patted the long face, then fitted the bridle swiftly, grabbed the reins, and swung onto the animal's bare back. It was not easy getting a solid grip with his knees on the animal's flank, but he often rode his father's horses bareback. It was how he learned to ride, as a matter of fact.

Digging his heels into the bay's flanks, he set off for the high country through the swiftly falling darkness. Billy hoped for a moon—and that he would not get lost. Only twice before had he ridden with his father to the Double Bar.

Ryan was shaking Cole gently by the shoulder. Cole looked up at the man's face bent over him in the dim bunkhouse. A patch of moonlight was filtering in through a window behind Ryan. From the slant of the light, Cole guessed it was well after midnight.

"You figure anyone's on your trail, Cole?"

Cole sat up quickly. "Hell, yes. Danny Larn most likely."

Ryan nodded. "That's why Blue put me on watch. There's a horse and rider crashing about on the ridge above us. Could be one of Larn's men who's lost his way in the dark."

"I'll get dressed."

"Blue's ridden up there to investigate."

As Cole pulled on his Levi's and reached for his gunbelt, he heard two horses riding into the yard.

"I'll see," said Ryan, slipping quickly out the bunkhouse door. Cole already had his hat on. Now he pulled on his boots, cursing. A second later he was on his feet, darting through the doorway into the cool night.

In the light of a lantern held by Nancy, Cole saw Billy Thomaris slip slowly off the bare back of Cole's bay. Blue helped the boy stay on his feet, and as the boy staggered wearily, Nancy hung the lantern on a nail driven into the porch post and hurried down the steps to stand beside Billy.

Blue glanced at Cole as Cole hurried into the pool of light. "Billy came to warn you, Cole. Danny Larn's been at the Flying O. Seems like he beat up Billy's father some and even slapped his mother around before he was able to get Zeke to tell Larn where you'd ridden to."

Billy, tears streaming down his face, looked unhappily up at Cole. "He told me to stay in the barn, Cole, and then to ride and warn you when I got the chance."

"So you saw the whole thing," Nancy said softly, her hand resting lightly on the boy's tousled head.

He looked at her and nodded miserably. "I wanted to help Pa. I wanted to really bad, but he told me to stay in the barn and wait to warn Cole. I hate those men, Nancy. I hate them!"

Nancy opened her arms to the boy. He buried his face against her and sobbed out his misery. As she consoled the boy, she looked around at the men. "I guess we know now which side we're on—if we ever doubted it for a minute before this."

Ryan nodded sadly, as did Blue.

"Seems to me like they'll camp for the night before pushing on up here. And they might have trouble finding the place." Cole said. "But I think we should be waiting for them come morning."

"We will," said Blue.

Nancy quieted Billy and led him into the ranchhouse. "You must be famished," she told him.

The boy looked forlornly back at the men. "I got lost or I would've got here sooner."

"Any riders behind you?" Cole asked.

"None that I could hear."

"You get some food in you and then get some sleep," Ryan said to Billy. "You done fine."

That seemed to make Billy feel much better. He brightened somewhat and followed Nancy into the ranchhouse.

Cole turned to Ryan. "How many men does Larn have?"

"Four, as mean a band of hardcases as I've seen in a long time. Those men weren't hired, they were trapped. One of them, the feller Larn seems to rely on the most, is a tall, bony drink of water who's dyin' on his feet. Consumption. Talk in town is he's as mean as Larn—figures he don't have much to lose at this stage, I guess."

"What's his name."

"Miles Crocket, I hear tell. I only saw them that once when they pulled up in front of Stitch's barber shop."

Cole nodded. "So it's five men, all told. And there's three of us."

"No, four," said Nancy from the doorway.

They all looked up at her. "No, sir!" said Blue.

Nancy laughed. "Who do you think you're giving orders to, young 'un? You may be taller than I am, but I remember the day you was born."

"You already got shot up once today," Cole said mildly.

The two men smiled at that and Nancy looked suddenly at Cole, her face darkening. "That was pure luck, mister."

"Yes, it was Cole admitted. "But sometimes I'd rather be lucky than rich."

"I'm going with you. And that's settled."

"Yes, Nancy," Ryan said with a deep sigh. "I sure wish you could shoot straight."

With a derisive laugh, she turned on her heels and disappeared back into the ranchhouse to see to Billy. Smiling slightly, Blue looked at Cole.

"We'll have four guns, then. And sis is one hell of a shot, Cole. You sure as hell *was* lucky this afternoon."

"I know it," said Cole. "She admitted she was only firing over my head to warn me off. Thing was, I didn't know that."

"She won't be firing over anyone's head tomorrow," said Blue. "Let's go into the bunkhouse and get this surprise party set up."

Cole said, "You understand Larn's the law now. When I rode up here I did not mean to ask you to go against the law."

"We know that," said Ryan, his round face serious. "But you couldn't keep us out of this now if you wanted to—not after what Billy just told us."

"We're in, Cole," said Blue emphatically. "All the way."

"Thanks."

As Cole followed the two men into the bunkhouse, he shook his head. Events were obviously spinning out of control, and there seemed no way he could get a handle on it. He slumped down on his bunk and watched Ryan light the coal-oil lamp hanging from a ceiling beam. This was what happened when two powerful forces clashed, he realized, and found himself wondering how many small ranchers—like the Doblers here and Thomaris—had suffered as a result of his father's lust for land over the years.

Perhaps this was why Cole was unable to get a single one of his father's fellow cattlemen to throw in with him against Harris—and why it was just the Circle C that had confronted Poole when he came to serve that court order. The thought sobered Cole and he wondered miserably if this vendetta with Harris and his hired killers—all the torment and bloodshed it had caused—was to be the only lasting legacy bequeathed him by his father.

"You with us, Cole?" Blue asked, a faint smile on his face.

Cole smiled back at the man and leaned forward. "Sure," he said. "Just letting my thoughts run away with me was all."

"Yeah," said Blue sympathetically. "I can understand that. Things are really piling up fast, looks like. Why not let Ryan and me set this up? We know this high country like the back of our hands. We won't have no trouble fixin' this surprise for Larn and his men."

"That's a fine idea. Let's hear what you've got in mind."

When the three finished making their plans an hour later, Cole suggested he take the next watch. There was no argument to that and as Cole passed the ranchhouse a few moments later, he noticed the lamps inside were out, which meant that Nancy and Billy were getting some needed sleep.

He pulled the collar of his sheepskin coat up around his neck and started climbing for the ridge over the ranch, glad for the chance to do something, since sleep for him now was out of the question.

He found himself wondering when he would be able to sleep again—really sleep.

Six

AS THE MORNING mists slowly lifted from Razorback Ridge, the four carefully settled themselves into their assigned emplacements.

Cole had been stationed at the northernmost and highest lift of the ridge. Next to him, at least fifty yards further along the rocky spine, Blue was making himself comfortable behind a boulder that gave him a clear view of the flat below.

Ryan was next, another twenty to thirty yards along, squeezed in between two monumental rock faces. He too had an unobstructed view of the flat. A hundred yards to the south and at the ridge's highest outcropping in that direction, Nancy was getting herself comfortable beside a jack pine that gave her a poor view of the trail as it left the flat and climbed the ridge, but which was nevertheless a perfect spot from which to direct a deadly enfilade on any of Larn's men who might make it to the ridge.

Nancy had insisted from the beginning, however—and Cole had backed her all the way—that they were not to open fire without first warning Larn and his men. Since Cole made it clear that he was willing to be brought in, but not by Larn, they agreed he would tell Larn this and propose that the Doblers be the ones to take him in. If Larn would agree to that and would return with his men back the way they had come, Cole would promise to be in Broken Bow by four that afternoon.

If Larn refused to accept this deal, it would serve as proof positive that Larn had no intention of bringing in Cole alive. The way in which he brought Gunnison and Pete Anton into Broken Bow had convinced Cole of this already; but there was always the chance, he realized, that Gunnison or Pete—or both of them—had tried to get cute with Larn and had drawn on him. Cole doubted this strongly, yet he had to allow for that possibility, at least.

The first rays of the morning sun had burnt off the last traces of mist still hugging the flat when the sound of shod hooves crossing stony ground echoed along the ridge. Cole had already levered a fresh cartridge into his Winchester. Now he leaned out just a little, straining to get a better view of the flat.

A dark line of horsemen moved out of the timber on the far edge of the meadowland. Cole squinted carefully. There were five horsemen. The lead rider was wearing a light Stetson and was dressed in a dark suit. The rider closest to him—a couple of horse-lengths back—was wearing a buckskin jacket. A flop-brimmed hat was pulled low over his face. He rode tall, somewhat jerkily, in the saddle. From Ryan's description of Larn and Miles Crocket—and from Billy's own account that morning before they rode out—

this was Danny Larn in the lead with his lieutenant just behind him.

Cole's fingers sweated against the wood of the Winchester's stock. The sun peeped over the mountains behind the ridge and found the back of his neck. Blue was right. They would be defending the ridge with the sun at their back and with Larn and his men having to squint into it.

The riders crossed the meadow swiftly, strung out in a ragged line, Larn still well in front. Soon they seemed to be coming awfully fast. They hammered toward the foot of the ridge, their coats streaming out behind them, each rider clearly distinguishable from the other. It had been decided that Cole would call out when the first rider reached a stunted jack pine halfway up the trail. Cole watched as Danny Larn neared this tree. As soon as the man's horse labored past it, Cole pointed his rifle at the sky and fired. Larn pulled up quickly.

As the rifle's sharp report echoed over the ridge, Cole got to his feet and stood in plain sight. "Hold it right there, Larn," Cole called down to him.

Larn tugged his flat brim down further to shield his eyes from the bright sun. With obvious difficulty he caught sight of Cole. Sitting his horse quietly, he made no move for his gun, while the fellow in the buckskin jacket reined up beside him. Larn said something to his deputy, and the fellow turned in his saddle and gestured to the rest of the riders, causing them to hang back.

"You're firing on the law, Cole," Larn called up the slope. "That makes you an outlaw!"

"That was just a warning shot, Larn. To get your attention."

"Well, you got it."

"I'm not going in with you, Larn. I don't like the odds of my reaching Broken Bow alive in your care. I'll give myself up—when I'm ready."

Larn took no offense at the implication in Cole's words. In fact, he appeared to accept it quite matter-of-factly. "You mean you'll come in alone—on your own."

"The Doblers will bring me in. If, that is, you turn around and take your men off their land and go back the way you came. You can figure I'll be in Broken Bow as soon as I can manage it."

At Cole's mention of the Doblers, Larn started, aware for the first time that he was under more than one gun. At once his eyes searched the rocks for sign of those other guns. He gave it up after a few moments, snugged his hat down, and tipped his head to get a better view of Cole.

"I don't make deals, Cole. Not with an outlaw."

"Have it your own way."

"On the other hand, maybe we could work something out." The man's thin line of a mouth lengthened into what was supposed to be a smile. "So let's dicker." As he spoke, Larn gently urged his mount further up the trail toward Cole.

"Hold it right there, Larn."

But Larn kept going up the steep incline. "I'm sick of shouting and staring up into that damned sun. Now, I'm willing to turn back if you'll let me leave one of my men here with you. Kind of an insurance policy. I'd look pretty silly if I turned back on your word alone—and you kept right on running."

"I said hold it, Larn. And I meant it."

Larn kept coming. Cole aimed quickly and fired, putting a round just over Larn's head. From the look on the man's face, Cole knew Larn had heard the slug as it burned through the air a few inches above his hat.

Larn pulled up, his face suddenly hard. "Damn you, Randall. Put up that rifle and let's talk like sensible men. Either that or we'll shoot it out with you and the Doblers. But hell, man, how many more people you going to drag into this business? Ain't you sick of leaning on others?"

What Larn said cut into Cole cruelly as he realized the indisputable truth of it. With the shrewd insight of a devil the man had touched a sore point that Cole himself had been probing restlessly all during the morning watch as he went over in his mind what Zeke Thomaris and his wife—and Billy—had gone through for his sake.

"All right then," Cole said wearily. "Talk."

"Sure, Randall. But I don't like this squinting into the sun. Let me get off my horse and walk up a ways to meet you. You can come down and meet me halfway, at least."

Cole nodded. "All right."

Larn swung carefully off his mount. The man seemed extraordinarily meticulous in the way he picked his way up the steep, rocky slope. He appeared particularly unwilling to reach out and grab anything with his hands to steady him. He was fearful, Cole realized, of soiling his hands.

Cole slanted down the slope toward Larn, his rifle held ready in his right hand, his finger resting lightly on the trigger. There was a fresh round in the firing chamber and the safety was off. Less than ten yards from each other both men pulled up.

Larn looked quickly about him, found a polished stone shouldering out of the slope, and sat down upon it, but not before brushing it lightly with his hands. As soon as he was comfortable, he looked over at Cole. "Much better," he said. "That damn sun was a nuisance."

Cole remained standing, his rifle still loosely trained on Larn.

"Do I have to talk to you down the length of a gun barrel? What kind of a man are you, Randall, to treat the law this way."

"You're scum, Larn. And a cold-blooded murderer. Don't call yourself the law. You said you had a deal. You said you wanted to leave one of your men here as insurance. That sounds reasonable."

"And it is—very reasonable." Larn looked back down

the slope. "See that tall, skeletal rider in the deerskin jacket? His name's Miles Crocket. He's dying of consumption, he is, and he's so close to death he has conversations with him every night before he goes to sleep." Larn laughed softly. "Miles don't care what happens to himself—just so long as he doesn't die in bed coughing his lungs into a puddle."

Cole had glanced down the slope for just an instant, his attention focusing on the rider Larn described. Before he looked back at Larn, he caught a sudden movement out of the corner of his eye and swung back to Larn in time to see the man's gun hand come up with a gleaming six-gun, the muzzle holding steady on Cole's midsection.

Cole swore softly, furiously at himself.

Larn smiled. "All right, cowboy. Drop that rifle and tell your friends in the rocks if they fire on me you're a dead man. Go on. Do as I say."

"You talk too much, Larn. But I'm not listening anymore."

As Cole spoke he leaped sideways, brought his rifle up, and pumped a slug at Larn. He got off two more quick shots while scuttling, crablike, to the protection of a low cluster of boulders. Both shots had gone high as Larn ducked behind the rock he had been sitting on. But Larn recovered quickly and sent two quick shots after Cole. As Cole took cover behind the boulders, he heard the slugs whispering over his shoulders.

Keeping low, he heard the Doblers opening up from above him. He chanced a look down the slope and saw Larn scrambling down the incline, ducking from tree to bush, while his men flung themselves from their saddles and started racing up the slope, guns blazing.

The fire from Larn's men was so concentrated that Cole had no choice but to keep his head down, and the fire from Blue and Ryan seemed to have little effect on Larn's men as they kept low and moved with catlike speed up the slope, closing fast on Cole's position. Realizing he was too far down the slope, Cole left the protection of the rocks and darted up the steep incline toward a small stand of pine. Bullets buzzed like angry wasps about him, but he made it to the pines and flung himself to the ground behind one of the trees.

Poking the muzzle of his rifle out through a low cover of brush pine, he drew a bead on one of Larn's men and squeezed off a shot. The fellow grabbed at his thigh and pitched backward, screaming. Then he began tumbling down the slope, still screaming.

At this the firing from Larn's men grew less spirited. At last it ceased entirely, and as the echoes of the gunfire faded, all Cole could hear was the cursing and moaning of Larn's deputy as the fellow continued his helpless rolling slide down the steep slope.

"'That's enough!" cried Larn.

Cole saw Larn getting to his feet then, a white handkerchief in one hand, his gleaming Smith & Wesson in the other.

"Give us safe passage back down this ridge!" Larn demanded. "I got a wounded man to take care of!"

Cole stood up cautiously, his rifle tucked under his chin, the Winchester's sights centering on Larn's chest. "Get out of here, Larn! Go on back the way you came, and don't waste any time about it!"

Larn nodded agreeably and holstered his revolver. As he was about to turn around and start down the slope, Nancy screamed, "Look out, Cole!"

Cole spun and dove back behind the pine as a shadowy figure just above him loosed two quick shots at him. The slugs pounded dirt at Cole's feet. Cole brought up his rifle and squeezed off a shot at the figure. But he was too late as the man vanished over the ridge, to be followed almost immediately by another one of Larn's deputies.

"We're outflanked!" Cole cried up at the Doblers. "Get the horses!"

Jumping to his feet, Cole saw Larn scrambling on down the slope toward his horse. Cole levered another round into the Winchester's firing chamber, aimed, and fired at him. But the footing under Cole was loose and the shot went high. Larn swung onto his horse and plunged precipitously down the slope, the tall consumptive he called Miles negotiating the steep, loose ground just ahead of him, both men punishing their horses severely.

Cole fired once more, then gave it up as a bad job and scrambled back up to the crest of the ridge. Ryan had already gone for the horses and was riding toward him, leading their horses. Nancy and Blue were running toward Cole.

"Keep down, Ryan!" Cole called. "Keep down!"

But Ryan just clapped spurs to his mount and kept coming. He was pulling up, getting ready to throw Cole the reins to his horse when two shots cracked out of the timber beyond the ridge. Ryan slapped his left hand over his right shoulder and spilled backward off his horse.

"Down! Down!" Cole cried to Nancy and Blue as they raced up.

But Nancy paid no attention as she rushed past Cole to Ryan's side. Cole had heard Ryan hit the ground and was sure the man had missed striking any of the many boulders that poked up out of the broken terrain. Keeping her head down, Nancy comforted Ryan as best she could. Ryan was conscious. Cole could hear Nancy speaking to him as he kept himself down and peered warily into the timber.

Blue, crouching low, stopped for a while beside Nancy and Ryan, then darted over to where Cole was crouching.

"He'll be all right," said Blue. "The bullet passed on through the fleshy part. But he's going to feel it for a while."

"We've got to get him out of here now," said Cole.

He glanced back down the slope. Larn and Miles Crocket were at the foot of the ridge now, riding onto the flat. As Cole watched, he saw Larn ride right past his wounded deputy, heading north.

"There's a narrow trail a few miles north of here," Blue said, watching them ride off also. "They can use that to outflank us."

"And those other two are safe now in the timber. They'll pick off our horses soon if we don't move out fast."

Blue nodded. "You got any ideas?"

"Yes. I'll mount up and ride south to that trail you mentioned. I'll wait for Larn there, and give him a run for his money. Maybe I can lose him in the Sawtooths. It's me he wants, not the Doblers."

"That's too dangerous, Cole. Soon's you get on your horse, they'll pick you off."

"Maybe. But pinned down here, we're just sitting ducks waiting for Larn and his men to reach us. As soon as I'm out of sight, you and Nancy better take Ryan back to the ranch. You might need to take him into Broken Bow later."

Cole turned then and keeping low with his rifle at the ready, ran toward the horses. They had pulled up about ten yards farther along the ridge. As Cole ran, a shot from the timber struck a boulder just in front of him, causing a stinging shower of rock fragments to pepper his face. He flung up his arm to shield his eyes and kept going. Blue then began giving him covering fire, opening up a brisk fusillade on the timber.

Reaching his horse, he flung his Winchester into the boot, grabbed the trailing reins, and swung into his saddle. Another shot from the timber hummed over his head as he clapped spurs to the roan. Glancing to his left Cole saw two shadowy figures racing along through the woods, trying to keep up with him.

Bending low over the horse's neck, Cole turned his horse and galloped straight for the timber—and the running figures. He knew the chance he was taking, but they would be firing at him through trees, and he would be coming at them head-on, giving them a much smaller target. Two more shots rang out from the timber as he rode closer. Both rounds missed. A third shot went wild when the slug clipped off a branch at the edge of the clearing.

By that time Cole was at the timber. Drawing his Colt, he flung himself from his horse and charged deeper into the woodland. A bright patch of shirt caught his eye and he fired, heard a squeal of pain, then sent another shot at the fleeing shadow. The bullet whined off a tree. Cole caught a glimpse of another running figure and sent two quick shots after it. This one went down. Cole fired again, aiming lower. The man scrambled to his feet and plunged frantically deeper into the timber.

Cole pulled up. The sound of the two men crashing through the underbrush grew rapidly fainter. He listened for a moment longer, then left the timber. Snatching up the reins to his horse, he waved to Nancy and Blue, and mounted up.

A moment later they were out of sight behind him as he rode north along the ridge to meet Larn. There would be no fool palaver this time. He would let Larn get a good look at him—then draw him and his deputies after him as far as he could from the Double Bar. The Doblers had already paid dearly for their part in Circle C's private war with the railroad, and Cole was sick of dragging others into his troubles.

No more, he told himself. *No more. From here on you go it alone. You fight your own battles.*

As soon as Cole was out of sight, Nancy turned to Blue, who was helping her lift Ryan to his feet. "What's Cole up to, Blue?"

Blue, intent on helping Ryan make it to his horse, muttered, "He's going to draw Larn and his men off so we can get back to the ranch with Ryan." Blue glanced at Nancy. "I think we should take him in to see Doc Wilder. We'll have to use the buckboard. He won't be able to ride a horse that distance."

Nancy nodded. "You're right. But I'm thinking of Cole.

If he plays it too close, he's liable to get himself killed—legally."

Ryan was cursing softly and his face was unpleasantly sallow. But he had heard what they were saying about Cole. As Blue heaved his chunky brother up into his saddle, Ryan said, "You can't let Cole do that."

As Blue passed the reins up to Ryan, he looked at Nancy. "He's right. We can't. Like you say, he might get himself killed. But the odds are two to one now instead of five to one. We've done all we could. It's Ryan we got to worry about now."

Nancy nodded and started for her horse. Blue was right, of course. Getting her wounded brother into Broken Bow for expert medical attention and seeing to it that Billy Thomaris got safely back to his ranch, these were what they had to worry about now—not Cole Randall. Nevertheless, as she mounted up and waited for Blue and Ryan to catch up to her, she could not dismiss the nagging sense that she could not ignore Cole's danger.

"Those two in the woods," Nancy said, as her brothers caught up to her. "Do you think Cole gave them enough of a scare?"

Blue shrugged. "Whether he did or not, their horses are still at the foot of the ridge—and that wounded deputy is still down there. Larn just rode off and left him."

"Which means we'll have them two at our backs as soon as they gather their wits and go back down for their mounts." Nancy pulled up. "Blue, do you think you can handle Ryan alone?"

Blue kept going and looked back at her. "What is it, sis?" he asked. "You got somethin' cookin' in that head of yours. Out with it."

"I'm going back down there and loose those horses—and see to that wounded deputy."

Blue pulled up. Ryan, cursing softly, reined in also. "Are you, now," said Blue.

"If that deputy dies, it'll be on our heads as well as

Cole's. And if those two in the timber get their horses, we'll likely have trouble making it to Broken Bow with Ryan. I don't see as we got much choice in the matter."

Blue sighed. "Okay, sis. Just be careful, that's all."

"You just get Ryan into Broken Bow—and see to Billy. His folks must be worrying about him."

Blue nodded and waved. Ryan turned and smiled crookedly at her. Then he turned back around and concentrated on staying on his horse. The bandanna she had snugged around the wound was now dark with his blood. For a moment Nancy wondered if she was doing the right thing, but only for a moment. She peeled her horse around and rode back along the ridge.

Pulling up a moment later, Nancy looked over and caught sight of three saddled horses grazing in a bunch at the edge of the flat and what appeared to be the sprawled body of the wounded deputy. The man was at the foot of the slope, stretched out with his back propped against a pine.

She continued on for a hundred yards or so until she found the trail leading down to the flat, then gave her mount its head and started down. When she reached the flat, she cut back until she reached the wounded deputy. She approached him with her Colt drawn. He was conscious and had twisted around, his own gun in his hand.

Nancy pulled up about ten yards from him, her revolver trained loosely on the deputy. "You want to throw that gun aside?"

He swallowed, looked at her for a moment, then tossed his revolver a few feet from him and leaned his head back against the tree, breathing heavily.

"I'm hurt bad," he said weakly, petulantly.

"And Danny Larn rode off and left you."

The man nodded glumly. "The son-of-a-bitch!"

Nancy holstered her gun and rode closer, studying the deputy. He was a fat, slovenly individual. Week-old dirt was caked on his neck and the backs of his hands. Long,

96

greasy hair, cut unevenly, hung down from under his misshapen, flop-brimmed hat. As an arm of the law, Nancy reflected, he didn't cut much of a figure.

"You people is goin' to pay for this," the fellow said sullenly, hopelessly.

"That's right," Nancy agreed. "What's your name, deputy?"

"Sandy Fremont."

"Well, Sandy, unbuckle your gunbelt and tell me which horse over there is yours."

"Hell!" the man said, his voice becoming a whine. "I can't ride with this busted leg! I'm wounded bad. I'm bleedin'!"

"Then you can lay there and bleed to death." Nancy started to pull her horse around.

"Wait! Wait a minute, for God's sake, woman!"

"You want to try riding into Broken Bow?"

The man moistened his cracked lips. "Where . . . where's your place?"

"You'll never find it in your condition. And if you showed up there, my brothers would shoot you on sight. Your best bet is Broken Bow or a friendly rancher between her and town." She paused. "I wouldn't stop at the Flying O if I were you, though."

The man looked quickly, guiltily away. Nancy wondered if this was one of the two men who had worked over Zeke and his wife. The thought disturbed her, filling her with sudden, conflicting emotions concerning this sullen, slovenly fellow whimpering before her.

"I haven't got the time for you, mister," Nancy told him bluntly. "I asked you before. Which is your horse?"

"The gray," he answered.

She dismounted, picked up the man's six-gun and stuck it into her belt, then waited for the man to struggle out of his gunbelt. When he had, she threw it well up the slope, remounted and rode over to the grazing horses, caught up with reins of the deputy's mount and led it back to the man. As she did so, she noticed the sawed-off shotgun in the saddle boot. A mean weapon. Pulling up in front of the deputy, she reached over and pulled out the shotgun, split it, and dumped the shells onto the ground. Then she dropped the shotgun back into the boot.

The deputy struggled unhappily, grudgingly, up onto one foot, holding on to the tree for support. Nancy dismounted and helped him toward his horse. He cried out like a little boy when he had to drag his wounded thigh over the cantle. As he settled into the saddle, he leaned far over the pommel and groaned, both hands clutching the saddle horn. Nancy heard him whining something about not being able to make it.

She stepped back. "You got them reins?"

He grabbed for them. "But . . . I ain't ready yet."

She slapped the gray's rump smartly and let out a short yell. The horse took off at a dead run. Fremont almost went tumbling back off the animal. He caught himself, however, and the gray settled into a ragged run. Nancy watched the deputy go, satisfied she had done her best for him and finding it difficult to care one way or the other.

She rode after the remaining horses then, snatched up their reins, and started off at an easy run along the base of the ridge. The corner of her eye caught the sudden glint of sunlight on metal. She turned in her saddle and saw the two deputies Cole had chased back into the timber scrambling down the slope toward the flat. One of them appeared to be limping badly. They could see she was taking their horses; and even as she watched, the healthy deputy pulled up, lifted his rifle to his shoulder, and squeezed off a shot. Nancy dug her spurs to her horse as the bullet sang harmlessly off a rock just behind her, and kept going until one of the mountain's shouldering walls came between her and the ridge.

Only then did she ease up. Her plan was to leave the

horses miles from the two deputies and then double back to the ranch. That was her intention. Only the further she rode, the less this plan satisfied her. Blue could take care of Ryan and Billy now. They didn't really need her. And if they didn't, perhaps Cole Randall might.

She liked Cole Randall. And that surprised her, since she had taken an instant dislike to his father, a man she had met one day last summer in The Lucky Lady.

"Take it easy, sis," said Blue. "You'll get served, all right."

The three of them had just created a small sensation by demanding that she be served. All she had wanted was to join her brothers in a beer, but the moment she entered the place, the room had grown ominously quiet. Every eye had watched her sit down with her brothers, and when Blue ordered the three beers from the barkeep the place had gone so silent that she could hear the sound of a wagon rattling by in the street and the sharp, clear shout of a schoolboy in the distance. The barkeep stood over them, at a loss.

Then Nancy saw the tall, powerful figure of Delmar Randall get up from his poker game and stride over toward them, intent on setting matters straight. Flinty eyes studied her coldly from under thick, gray eyebrows as he approached. The man's face was deeply seamed, the nose strong and powerfully hooked.

"This here establishment serves only men, ma'am," Randall said, his deep voice carrying to every corner of the room. "It's a cattleman's place. It ain't fittin' you be coming in here dressed like this."

"Dressed like this?"

The man frowned, his Olympian patience nearing its limit. "Dressed like a man, ma'am."

"I see. You would rather I dressed like the tarts." Her glance left him then and directed itself at the two bar girls

still hanging on the necks of their customers as they watched her, their long red gowns and off-the-shoulder blouses bright and gaudy invitations to drink and play. "You'd prefer me to dress like a whore."

The man straightened abruptly, massively affronted. When she saw the reaction, it made her laugh outright. It looked as if smoke would soon pour out of his ears and nostrils.

Blue spoke up then. "We're cattlemen, Randall. Nancy here is a full partner. We're the Doblers and we run the Double Bar outfit in the Sawtooths. You can serve us or throw us out—all three. Your choice."

"The Double Bar!" snorted Delmar Randall. "You call yourselves cattlemen, do you? The first good rain'll wash you off that range. You'd be better off herdin' mountain goats than cattle!"

The place seemed to jump at the sudden explosion of laughter that greeted Randall's contemptuous dismissal of them as cattlemen. Randall laughed as loud and as heartily as the rest. Indeed, the laughter seemed to placate the man, to give him the satisfaction his outrage demanded. With a negligent nod at the bartender, he returned to his poker game. It was his world and he had decided that Nancy might be served.

Now, thinking back on that day and remembering how Cole's father had acted toward her and her brothers, she found it difficult to explain the gentleness, the obvious concern for others, that motivated Cole. His father's strength was apparent in Cole's every line and action. He had the same impressive height, the broad shoulders and piercing eyes under the massive, broad brow, the riveting glance that caught and held, the effortless grace and ease of movement, the sense of hidden power. But nowhere in the son's makeup, it seemed, could she find the father's brutal, careless arrogance.

Nancy was still mulling over this curious fact ten miles further along when the broken remnants of the Sawtooth Ridge fell away behind her and she found herself riding up a narrow, rocky, shale-strewn trail. Half an hour later she reached a small meadow, a familiar mountain stream cutting swiftly through its northern reaches. Here, she decided, she would leave the horses.

She rode over to the stream with them, thought a moment, and then with a sigh dismounted and removed the saddles, dropping them in a heap under a small cottonwood. She wasn't happy about taking the time, but the horses would be saved from sore, blistered backs as a result of her action. She mounted up again and spurred her horse on across the tableland. She had reached the trail that led south to her ranch when she heard—coming from the rugged, pine-clad peaks to the north—the distant rattle of gunfire.

Seven

COLE HAD lagged purposely to make sure that Larn and his man were able to keep on his trail. On more than one occasion he had given them a clear shot as he crossed a ridge or a flat within sight of them.

But this he had not counted on. A few moments before, as his horse labored up a steep, boulder-strewn incline, he had caught sight of a long shadow just above him, outlined against the sky. As he snatched his rifle from its boot and slid quickly off the horse, the man fired. The round struck his horse in the neck and the animal went down heavily, squealing in panic. Before Cole could get off an answering shot, someone fired at him from below, shattering the rockface he was flattened against, peppering his face with tiny shards of rock. He went down on one knee and managed to get off a quick rifle shot at the fellow above him, who ducked quickly from view. Cole turned his fire then on whoever it was coming up the incline from below.

Now, after moving as far from the rockface as he could, he was crouched down behind a boulder, waiting. After a while he grew impatient and poked his head out to look around. Two shots—one from above and one from below—caused him to duck swiftly back.

Hell, he was caught between a rock and a hard place, for sure. Cursing himself for his carelessness in letting them get so close in the first place, he inched out from behind the boulder, keeping as low as a snake's belly, and began to pull himself up the incline toward a looming boulder, one that was close enough to a rock wall to protect his back. As he reached it and ducked in behind it, another shot—this one from below—slammed up at him, ricocheting off the boulder. He kept low, grimacing as the rock fragments dug at his neck and face.

He dropped still lower and waited patiently. At last he saw Larn's light Stetson—just the top of it—moving out from behind a rock. Carefully, Cole pulled his rifle up to his shoulder and sighted. As soon as Larn's face appeared, he squeezed the trigger. Larn ducked back as the bullet gouged a white scar in the face of the rock behind which Larn still crouched. Cole swore at his poor shooting. Two quick shots came at him from above then, and he had to flatten himself to escape the withering fire.

He tried to pull himself around to direct some fire at the skyline, but his position was so miserably cramped, he simply could not manage it. He got off an awkward, hopeless shot in the direction of the ridge's crest, but it was at best a holding operation. As Cole saw it, the end of this miserable business was certain; the time he had left minimal. He glanced down the slope for more sign of Larn and was just in time to see him slip out from behind his boulder to a gully a lot closer to Cole. Using his six-gun, Cole sent a couple of shots over Larn's head so the man would know he had been seen. But this, also, Cole knew, was only a stopgap measure.

They were closing in.

He heard sudden, violent coughing coming from above. The draw echoed with its sound. Listening carefully, Cole got a much clearer idea of where Larn's man was coming from. He was close along the wall. The fellow had gone around and was inching down from almost directly above, which meant Cole was caught directly between the two.

Glancing back down the slope, he caught a glimpse of Larn getting ready to leave his spot. His head was down, but a portion of his left foot braced against a rock and a neat slice of his backside was barely visible. Cole aimed his six-gun at the target and squeezed off a shot. He had little hope of doing much more than discouraging Larn. Cole heard the bullet whine off a rock and saw Larn hurl himself back into the gully and out of sight.

Cole moved out from the wall, and facing the wall above him, wedged his back against the boulder and brought up his Winchester. If Larn popped out now, Cole would be a sitting duck, but Cole was counting on Larn to play it more cautiously than that. The coughing from above had ceased. Cole waited. He saw a few dislodged pebbles bouncing down the slope toward him. His finger tightened on the trigger as he brought the barrel up.

A tall, lanky shadow pushed out from the rock face. Cole swung the barrel up a mite higher and a cadaverous, bony face appeared in his sight. But even as he squeezed the trigger, the fellow ducked swiftly back into the shadows. Levering another shell into his firing chamber, Cole cursed and flattened himself against the wall.

A furious, sustained fusillade was then directed at Cole, causing Cole to have to screw his eyes shut to keep out the tiny splinters of rock that pelted him. Abruptly, the firing ceased and Cole took the opportunity to look out from behind the boulder, down the slope. Larn was moving closer. Cole fired at him with his six-gun. The slugs chewed up the ground at his feet and then Larn, a good ten yards closer, was behind another boulder.

Cole looked back up behind him, expecting fire from that quarter. But as the sound of his own gunfire faded, he could hear clearly the hacking, disabling cough of Larn's deputy.

What the hell! Cole thought. *Now's as good a time as any!*

He jumped out from behind the boulder and began racing up the steep slope toward the spot from within which the sound was coming. As Cole neared the place, he saw that the deputy had found a cleft in the rock wall. Cole charged for it, his rifle at the ready.

Before he reached the opening in the wall, the coughing within stopped. The sound of his boots digging into the loose soil—and that of his labored breathing—seemed to fill the universe with sound. Cole heard the man scrambling toward the cleft's entrance and from down the slope behind Cole came Larn's sudden shout of warning.

The deputy appeared before Cole, a startled look on his pallid face. As he started to bring up his six-gun, Cole fired. The shot was high, however, and all the round did was lift off the man's hat. Cole clawed leather, but before he could get his six-gun out, he heard a shot from below and felt the side of the mountain collapse on his head.

Cole clawed at the rock wall for support. A livid light had fallen over the world. His legs turned to rubber as he slowly sagged onto his knees, gasping for breath. It felt as if his head had grown to an enormous size. He reached up his hands to it, but there was nothing he could do as he toppled to the ground. The palms of both hands came away slick with blood.

He lay on his side, his eyes still open, still looking at a world on fire. The tall deputy was standing over him. Cole supposed the man was smiling. And then a shadow appeared on the ridge line above the deputy. A shot rang out, sounding as if it had been fired from the far end of a long pipe.

The deputy ducked away. Distant shouts came to him then. He heard feet scrambling and felt as well as heard gunfire just behind him. The shadow on the ridge disappeared as whoever it was started down the slope, still firing. Cole tried to raise himself onto his elbows, but the effort was too much. . . .

The slope spun sickeningly under him. He felt himself falling. Only dimly did he feel the gentle hands that lifted him by the shoulders and pulled him into the cleft. . . .

"Cole! Listen to me! Cole, listen!"

He did not want to. He wanted only to push away the emerging light, to fall back into the blessed darkness that cradled him. But the light increased its terrible intensity, and with it the awesome pounding in his head. . . .

"Cole! Please, Cole!"

The urgency in the voice calling him was like an ache he could not ignore. He opened his eyes and found himself astride a horse, his feet lashed firmly to the stirrups, an early-morning sun peering at him through cottonwoods, a bright stream winking back the sunbeams—like tiny knives. He turned his head and saw Nancy.

He tried to say something, but the words would not come. In addition to the terrible pounding in his head, there was the awesome dryness in his mouth and lips. He had the feeling that if he moved them in speech, they would crack open. He closed his eyes to escape the harsh light, then opened them again.

"That's better, Cole!" Nancy said, enormously heartened. "You've got to stay conscious or you'll fall off the horse!"

He tried to moisten his lips with his tongue, but the effort was futile. She saw at once his problem and reached back to her own mount for her canteen. She quickly unscrewed it and held its neck to his lips, gently tipping back his head. The cold water trickled into his mouth and down his throat. It had the revivifying effect, almost, of a shot of whiskey.

"Fine," he croaked hoarsely, when she pulled the canteen away. "Much better." He tried a shaky grin. "Why the hell ain't I dead?"

She smiled in sudden relief as she put the cap back onto the canteen. "Because you got solid rock for a head, I reckon. That bullet tore a hole in your scalp and maybe rattled a few bolts loose inside, but it didn't get inside as far as I can see, just ricocheted off."

"I got one mean helluva headache." Through slitted eyes he looked carefully around, as he babied what felt like the granddaddy of all hangovers. "How'd you get me here?"

"I lugged you onto my horse and then walked you this far. But I'm bushed, Cole. This here horse belonged to one of them deputies. I took it for safe keeping and left it here. I figure you can use it now, while I ride alongside."

He grinned at her carefully. "That should beat walking."

"You need a doctor to look at that head. Shall I take you to Broken Bow?"

"No. To the Circle C. Consuelo can handle this. And . . . you don't need to take me. I'll make it."

"Sure," Nancy said, swinging into her saddle. "Sure. Hang on now." She had hold of his mount's reins and with a concerned frown on her face urged her horse to an easy walk, pulling Cole's horse along behind her.

As soon as his horse started, Cole felt himself begin to fall. He grabbed hold of the saddle horn and tried to settle his feet more solidly into the stirrups. But there was no strength left in his thighs, and he saw then the wisdom of Nancy tying his feet securely. He could not fall off the horse; he could only hang on and try to ride as lightly as possible. After a while he found that the best way to ride was leaning over the pommel, his head down.

Shifting curtains of darkness swept sporadically across his field of vision. At first he thought it was low-flying buzzards or clouds. Then he realized the darkness was coming from within him. He closed his eyes and hung on, the jarring impact of each hoof a slow, building agony as his headache grew in ferocity—and in time with the hoofbeats.

He lost track of time, but somehow he kept his hands frozen to the saddle horn, every muscle in his body seeming to concentrate on that single effort. The muscles in his arms and shoulders seemed to have become transformed into rigid steel cables. Occasionally he became aware of the sun's changing position in the heavens above him. At last he felt the sun's rays moving in under the brim of his hat, prying into his tightly shut eyes, probing with painful fingers into the awesome cauldron that was his head.

He began to lose consciousness for longer and longer times, being drawn from the sweet oblivion only when the horse's pace quickened or slackened as he negotiated particularly difficult terrain. He came to associate the feel of grass turf under the horse's hoofs with sleep and relief from pain, the rattle of gravel and shale and the click of shod hooves against stone with a weary pull back to consciousness.

But he hung on, even as they rode into real darkness. . . .

The voices of Fiddle and Gus hauled him back to reality. He felt their strong hands helping him inside. They turned him and he plunged backward onto the bed. But the moment his head came down, a light exploded deep within his skull and he heard a groan wrench itself from his parched throat. Hurried hands rolled him onto his side.

He was aware of someone bending over him.

"Cole!"

He opened his eyes just a little. There was a lamp on the table. The sudden brightness of it caused him to squeeze shut his eyes again. But in that brief glimpse of the room he saw Nancy standing by the door, her hat in her hand, watching. And Fiddle standing nervously by her side. He opened his eyes a second time and saw that it was Gus who had called his name.

"Get . . . Consuelo," Cole said. "Where is she?"

"She's gone, Cole! She took a horse and lit out! She said she was going back to her people!"

Cole groaned.

"Get a doctor. Get Wilder. I want him to cut off this head." He tried to smile, but it was more of a grimace.

"I'll ride in and get him," said Nancy.

"No, I can do that," Gus said. "You ride to the Box W. and get Linda to come. She's fixed worse than this. She'll nurse him proper."

Cole watched her clap on her hat and leave the room. Gus turned back to Cole.

"You just rest up now, Cole. You're to home now."

Cole was too exhausted to reply, but the words comforted him. He closed his eyes and waited for the throbbing in his head to subside. It felt like Harris was laying track, finally, right through a tunnel in his head. Cole groaned softly at the thought.

That was probably just what that bastard was doing. . . .

While Nancy rode across the Box W compound, one of the windows in the first floor of the ranchhouse began to glow as a sulfur match was struck inside the room. A moment later a lantern was lit, then turned up brightly, sending a warmth of light out through the window and across the veranda. Nancy pulled up in front of the low veranda and waited.

The door opened and a man she vaguely recognized as Bill Graham stepped out onto the porch. He was dressed only in Levi's and a wollen undershirt, and was holding a rifle. A girl stood behind him in the doorway, carrying a lantern. That would be Linda, his daughter. Nancy had seen them once in Broken Bow, riding into town in their buckboard. The girl was a small, pretty thing, as she remembered.

"Hello, the house," Nancy called, quieting her horse.

Graham tipped his head in an effort to get a clearer view of Nancy in the darkness.

"I'm Nancy Dobler," she said. "The Double Bar. Gus Ames sent me. Cole's been hurt and he wants Linda."

Linda pushed out the door past her father, still holding the lantern. "Cole's hurt?" There was an anguish in her voice, a sense of despair that told Nancy at once just how important to this girl Cole Randall was.

"He got shot in the head," Nancy explained, "but the bullet just grazed him. He'll likely live, but he's sure got an awful headache and could use some tending to."

"I'll be ready in no time," she said, turning swiftly and hurrying back inside the ranchhouse.

"Light and rest," said her father. "I could rustle up some coffee while Linda's gettin' ready."

"Never mind," said Nancy, swinging out of her saddle and stretching her muscles wearily. "I'll just wait out here. Take less time."

"What happened, Nancy?" The man asked, stepping off the veranda and approaching her.

Nancy hesitated for only a second or two. "I found Cole wounded near our place."

"In the mountains."

"That's right."

"Now what in tarnation was he doing up in that country?"

"Earlier in the day he came up there to ask us to join up with him in his fight against Harris."

Graham was close enough now for Nancy to see his face clearly. The fellow frowned as he looked quickly at Nancy. "And did you?"

"Yes, we did."

"Well . . . that's fine. We're going to need all the help

111

we can get if we're going to stop Harris and that Danny Larn he's got installed as U.S. Marshal. You think it might have been Larn shot Cole?"

Nancy knew without a doubt it was Larn who had shot Cole. She had seen the whole thing. It was only because Larn and his deputy had concluded that Cole had been shot fatally that they had allowed her to drive them off. But she did not know how much she should tell Bill Graham—or anyone else, for that matter. Already, she and her brothers were in pretty deep with their open defiance of the law. She answered Graham cautiously.

"Likely it was Larn. He and his men were after Cole. They beat up on Zeke Thomaris and his wife the day before, they was that anxious to track Cole."

Graham considered a moment, his frown deepening. "You wait here, Nancy. I think I'll be going back with you and Linda. I want to talk to Cole as soon as he's able." He shook his head. "Then I'm going to ride into Broken Bow and see our lawyer. We've got to stop this man Larn—and soon. Things are gettin' out of hand."

Nancy watched Graham disappear into the house, a slightly ironic smile on her face. Yes, things were getting out of hand, all right, but it looked as if Cole would soon be in good hands. The question was, how long would Danny Larn and Maxwell Harris let him remain in Linda Graham's care?

Bill Graham and Linda rode over to the Circle C in the buckboard while Nancy rode alongside. Nancy was going back to Cole's ranch primarily to wait for the doctor Gus had ridden to Broken Bow to get. She was anxious to know about Ryan. She had not been too worried about her brother's wound, but she would feel a lot better when she heard what the doctor himself had to say.

The doctor drove into the Circle C compound a little before midnight. He was driving his mud-spattered buggy and seemed quite weary as he stepped down from it and hurried in to see Cole. He was with Cole a considerable time and when at last he left the bedroom and entered the kitchen, Nancy wasted no time in approaching him. She asked about Cole. After the doctor assured her that he would be all right, she asked about her brother.

The doctor was mopping his brow with a handkerchief, his long, deeply lined face grim, his eyes sunken into dark sockets. He looked at Nancy in surprise.

"Your brother?"

"Ryan Dobler."

"Oh, yes! I remember. A gunshot wound in the shoulder." He looked with suddenly narrowed eyes at Nancy. "Now that's a hell of a place to wound yourself cleaning a gun."

Nancy nodded grimly. "That's what happened, Doc."

"Yes . . . of course, of course."

"Will he be all right?"

"He'll be fine if he keeps the wound clean. I took out the bullet and cauterized the wound. He'll be wearing a sling for a couple of days; but outside of that, I see no problem."

"That's fine, Doctor. Thank you."

Nancy picked her hat up off the counter alongside the sink and put down the cup of coffee she had been sipping. She was tired and wanted to get back to the Double Bar before sunup.

"Just a moment, there," the doctor said as she turned to leave the kitchen.

She pulled up. Gus Ames and Fiddle turned to look at her curiously. They had been standing close to the bedroom door, peeking in at Cole. Nancy could just barely glimpse Linda bending over him. She appeared to be wiping off his forehead with a damp cloth. As the doctor had assured her, Cole was going to be all right.

"Yes, Doc?"

"What can you tell me about Cole's . . . accident?"

"Only what I told Bill Graham."

He frowned. "I see." His face was grim, his eyes seemed to have sunk deeper into their sockets. "Looks like this new U.S. Marshal is going to keep me pretty damn busy—either patching people up or burying them."

"Bill Graham said he's going in to Broken Bow to see a lawyer to stop Danny Larn."

The doctor slumped wearily into a chair at the table and shook his head. "A fat lot of good that'll do."

Nancy stood there in the middle of the kitchen looking at the doctor, then met the gaze of Cole's two old hired hands. She saw the same hopelessness in their eyes she had heard in the doctor's voice.

Abruptly, she turned and headed once again for the kitchen door.

"Nancy!"

She stopped in the doorway and looked back. Linda Graham was hurrying across the kitchen. Nancy waited on the porch as Linda hurried out to her.

"Before you go, I'd like to thank you," she said, "for helping Cole. The doctor says he has a concussion and perhaps a slight fracture."

"He'll be all right?"

"Yes. Thanks to you. But he would have died if you hadn't brought him here."

"Well, you take good care of him, Linda."

"Yes. I will."

Nancy smiled. "Good night. I have a long ride ahead of me."

"Oh, of course. Don't let me keep you any longer." Linda smiled tentatively. "Thank you again . . . so much."

Nancy pulled her hat down securely, turned, and walked off the low porch to her horse. As she stepped into the saddle, she looked back at Linda standing in the open doorway, and waved.

Then she turned her horse and clapped spurs to it. She

was at an easy lope as she cleared the gate and turned north toward the Sawtooths. She didn't like to admit it, but as she rode away from the ranch, she was aware of a vague sense of regret—of envy, even. And that really upset her. Why in hell should she be envious of that poor mousy little Linda?

And then, as the answer crowded in on her, she grew even more upset with herself and soon she had lifted her mount to a steady gallop as she swept across the moonlit grassland.

Linda watched Nancy ride off, her lips pursed thoughtfully. She had seen this Nancy Dobler only once before, on a weekend this past summer when she had gone to town with her father to do some shopping. Nancy had been with her two brothers then, and except for that part of her no clothes could change, she had acted and dressed as if she were not their sister, but their brother. Word had come back to Linda in the weeks that followed, word that astonished her. It seems that the Doblers had gone into The Lucky Lady where Nancy had demanded that she be served along with her brothers. She had stood up nicely to Delmar Randall in the bargain. That also had gotten back to Linda.

But despite the way Nancy Dobler carried herself and the way she dressed, she was a woman. There was no mistaking that. And a formidable one. Perhaps—in a land such as this, where the only law one could count on was the six-gun you strapped to your waist—Nancy Dobler was a woman better equipped than most to survive. Perhaps even better equipped than Linda.

But no, Linda told herself with sudden determination. She would not let herself believe that. She turned and hurried back into the ranchhouse. Once she reached Cole's side, she turned to her father sitting in a chair by the bed.

"As soon as we can move him," she said, "I want us to take Cole to the Box W."

Her father looked at her in surprise. But her tone allowed

no contradiction. He considered for just a moment or two, then nodded. "All right, Linda. Guess maybe we should, with Consuelo gone. Besides, it'll be a good idea to keep Cole out of sight. The doc thinks Larn might have left Cole for dead. If he did, we ought to let Larn think so for a while. Cole needs time now to mend." Linda's father got up then from the chair. "I'm going in to see Gus and Fiddle, and I just might remind the doc to keep his mouth shut."

As her father left the bedroom, Linda took a deep breath. She had not been too surprised to hear of Consuelo's departure. Linda had always felt that Consuelo felt more concern for Cole than for his father. With Cole a man now in full control of the Circle C, perhaps she felt her job was done. And it was! Linda felt a sudden, profound gratitude to the old Indian as she went back to placing damp compresses on Cole's head.

She had forgotten completely the despair she felt the day when Cole rode away from the Box W. There was still a chance for them both; she was sure of it now. As she laid a fresh compress gently down, smoothing Cole's hair back as she did, she was certain Cole smiled ever so slightly. That was enough for her. More than enough.

Linda felt almost giddy as she reached for another compress.

Eight

SIX DAYS later, on a Monday afternoon, Maxwell Harris was sitting at a poker table in The Lucky Lady contemplating a full house: kings and jacks. He had already bumped two players and Ross Grimsbee of the Lazy S was sitting across from him, eyeing the pot. He knew that Harris had drawn three cards. He had drawn only two. But Harris was sitting back, fire in his eyes—a look on his face that can only come with a full house or better.

"I'll stay with you, Max," Ross said wearily, pushing into the pot enough chips to cover the price of seeing what Harris had.

Harris was on the verge of raising the ante a bit more; it was table stakes, after all. But he thought better of it. He could afford to take it easy now, he realized. It wasn't as if Delmar Randall was about to stride into The Lucky Lady and lace Harris with his contempt. No, not a bit of it. That awesome, terrifying, humiliating nettle had been removed forever from under his saddle. It felt so good—so damn good!

With a magnanimous shrug Harris showed Ross his hand. Ross's eyebrows went up a notch as he acknowledged the superiority of Harris's cards. He shook his head and threw down his hand. "Hell, you must have drawn that."

"The two jacks and the king," Harris admitted, pulling in the chips.

Ross leaned back in his chair and stretched, tipping his head to look at the ancient wall clock beside the bar mirror. "Can't beat luck like that," he said, "and it's about time I moseyed on out to my cows."

He stood up, a rawboned, slit-eyed Texan with a lean, crooked jaw—made that way from too many barroom brawls. His icy blue eyes regarded Harris with the trace of a smile.

"You play poker some better without Randall to devil you, I notice. He was a real bull, wasn't he." It was not a question but a statement. "You bring that railroad through here, Max, and all will be forgiven. Hear?"

The other two players got up then, scooping up what meager chips they still possessed. There were slight smiles on their faces as they looked at Harris. They were smaller ranchers who knew precisely what Ross Grimsbee was driving at, and approved. It was a strange, electric moment for Harris as he realized what these three men were telling him: they would accept what had happened to Delmar Randall and the Circle C as long as the railroad went through and increased their prosperity. What they were also saying was that Delmar Randall had not meant all that much to them—that they had hated him as much as Harris himself had.

Of course they would never admit such a thing openly to Harris—or to anyone else for that matter. But it was plain enough to read in their faces and hear in their voices. Delmar

Randall had left a painful brand on all of them, it seemed.

Harris pushed his chair back and got to his feet, scooping his chips off the table and carrying them over to the bar.

"Drinks on me," he told the barkeep, slapping down his chips.

As the afternoon crowd scuffed hastily up to the bar, Harris strode out of The Lucky Lady. He felt good, really good, for the first time in a long time. The only cloud on his horizon was the fact that though Larn had searched now for the past five days, he had been unable to find Cole's body—or any trace of him. Larn had ridden back to where they had shot him and had found his blood-soaked hat. But that was the only trace Larn had found.

Larn was certain that Cole had been dragged off somewhere to die by whoever it was that had helped him. He was rotting in a shallow grave somewhere in the Sawtooths. That was Larn's conclusion, and it was one that Harris favored as well.

But Gus Ames and Fiddle were still out at the Circle C. still carrying on as if nothing had happened. Harris had driven out to the Circle C three days ago. There was no sign of Cole thereabouts, but Fiddle and Gus seemed to have the operation going along quite smoothly. It wasn't natural. And Harris had gotten the distinct impression that Gus and Fiddle knew something that Harris didn't—and that was fit to bust them wide open that they couldn't tell it.

Over the weekend Larn had scouted the ranchhouse with two of his men. He had returned last night weary of the vigil and absolutely certain that Cole was not on the ranch.

But it was just a cloud, really. Harris had learned that most of the ranchers in the valley had refused to join in Cole's protest against the railroad—that only the Box W, the Flying O, and a ratty little spread in the Sawtooths, the Double Bar, had consented to throw in with Cole. Though the Circle C's lawyer, Trace, was still making unfriendly noises, this was not an opposition capable of doing him much damage.

Harris was in the act of touching the brim of his hat to Mrs. Brineridge when he saw the two horsemen. He brought his heavy, thick-set body to a sudden halt—and swore. Mrs. Brineridge's face went white as she scuttled on past the banker, shocked right down to the laces on her high-topped shoes. But Harris paid no heed to the woman's sensibilities.

Cole Randall and Bill Graham were riding into Broken Bow. Rooted to the spot, Harris watched the two horsemen dismount in front of Eliot Trace's office and walk inside. The only indication that Cole had been wounded was the clean white bandage visible just under the sweat band of his dark Stetson—a new one, Harris realized.

Standing like that on the walk, impressive bulk a considerable obstruction, he was a nuisance, and as people walked around him, a few glanced questioningly at him. Harris saw this and rousing himself continued on to the bank. As soon as he entered it, he called one of his clerks over and told him to get Deal Wightman, that he would be waiting for the lawyer in his office. As the clerk hurried from the bank, Harris went into his office and walked quickly to his window.

He did not have long to wait. In a few minutes Eliot Trace left his office with Cole Randall and Bill Graham and crossed the street to Judge Warner's chambers. A small crowd had already gathered. Since last week, the wounding of Larn's two deputies and the speculation on Cole's death had been almost the sole topic of conversation in every saloon—and parlor—in the town.

Harris left the window and slumped down into his chair. With shaking hands he took a cigar from the humidor on his desk and lit it. He told himself that it was of no real importance that Cole Randall was alive. The other ranchers had, for the most part, abandoned him. And yet, no matter how often he repeated this to himself, he could gain no comfort at all from the assertion.

He knew what Cole and Eliot Trace were up to at that moment. Cole was giving himself up to be formally charged. Warner would set bail, Cole would pay it, and that would be that. No longer a fugitive from justice, Cole would ride out of Broken Bow and until the trial remain free to continue his intrigues against Harris—and the railroad.

The banker ground out his cigar into the ashtray on his desk. Where the hell was Deal Wightman? He got up suddenly and headed for the door—about to go after the lawyer himself—when it opened. The clerk looked in.

"Mr. Harris—maybe you better see this. . . ."

The fellow ducked so quickly back out the door that he knocked his green visor to one side. Harris hurried to the door and looked out. There was a small crowd on the boardwalk in front of the bank peering in through the open door. Cole Randall was at one of the teller's windows, counting out some money that had just been handed him by the teller. As Harris watched, Cole turned with the money and gave it to his lawyer standing beside him.

The amount for his bail, Harris had no doubt.

Cole looked up suddenly, saw Harris standing in the open doorway, and smiled thinly, coolly. The smile sent a shiver of apprehension down Harris's back. He recognized that smile and feared it—and for good reason: it was almost a duplicate of the smile Cole's father sometimes wore when he was rolling up his sleeves for trouble.

Harris stepped back quickly into his office and closed the door. Back behind his desk, he pulled out a fairly new bottle of scotch along with a glass. He poured himself a shot and downed it without caution, fighting panic. It was foolish, he knew, to see in Cole the same ruthlessness, the same unerring instinct for the jugular that his father possessed.

There was, after all, some of his mother in Cole's makeup. And that counted for something. Harris leaned back in his chair and closed his eyes and thought of Cole's mother. Both Harris and Delmar Randall had courted Mary Wills. This was before the bank, when Harris was selling hardware and dry goods where the hotel stands now.

Mary Wills was a small, delicate thing—a woman from St. Louis who had come West with her brother, only to see the man fail miserably as a shopkeeper and blow his brains out after incurring incredible gambling losses. Mary had become a seamstress then in order to make ends meet and Harris began courting her, since he had known her brother and had, toward the end, tried to help the man.

But his courtship had been tentative; his shyness was misinterpreted by Mary and laughed at by Del Randall, who overwhelmed her with attention and completely dominated her free time at the end of it; for once his intentions toward Mary Wills became known, there was not a single man in the territory prepared to go against the powerful rancher.

Except Harris.

And so, inevitably, they had fought for her—like two brute beasts they had come together one Saturday night outside the Grange hall where a dance was being held. The outcome of the fight was a foregone conclusion from the start. Harris knew he had no chance and Delmar Randall knew he could not lose to the smaller, less-muscular townsman.

Harris shook his head at the memory of it, hearing once again the shouts of the onlookers, seeing their faces livid in the lantern light, enduring their shouts of derision, their sporadic cheering whenever one or the other landed a blow. Most of the time the cheers were for Randall, not only because there were few in that crowd prepared to go against him, but also because Harris was so futile, so inept with his fists.

The memory of how poorly he had done that night still

twisted like a knife inside him whenever he recalled it. He had hoped to land a few punishing blows, nothing more. It was obvious Mary had already chosen, that—like everyone else in the territory, it seemed—she was afraid to refuse the man. Harris knew that. But the thought of it had driven him wild and all he had wanted was to make this man suffer somehow for what he was doing.

Only it was Harris who had suffered. For Delmar Randall it was a huge joke. He battered Harris with impunity and left him in the mud and walked in to Mary and the dance with insolent laughter on his lips—his face unscathed, his hair not even mussed.

From that time on he hated the man with a ferocity that made him physically sick at times. It ate away at him, like a worm that could not be satiated. And it grew not only worse, but intolerable when it became clear to everyone—including Mary—what a mistake she had made in marrying Del Randall. The harsh ranch life wore her down and Del's careless usage of her made it doubly insupportable. On more than one occasion she had let Harris know just how sorry she was for having allowed Del Randall to bully her into marrying him.

As the years wore on and Del Randall became all too certain how his wife felt about her marriage, the hatred between the two men became a corrosive, destructive force that poisoned the town and all those who knew them both. Though Mary openly admitted her love for Harris, she never allowed a single indiscretion to tarnish her marriage vows. Nevertheless, the knowledge of her lonely tragedy brought a miserable isolation to Harris and a tyrannical, but lonely power to Delmar Randall. For the man no longer bothered to temper his ambition with discretion. His furious recklessness grew more arbitrary with each passing season. All that he wanted, he took—as if daring the gods to strike him down.

Finally, with the death of Mary five years after Cole's

birth, the enmity was bonded and sealed to last throughout the lives of both men. It was that—Harris knew suddenly—and not the railroad that had brought Del Randall and himself to that confrontation a little more than a week ago when, after all these bitter years, he had raised his shotgun and waited exultantly for the old rancher to gallop closer . . . and still closer. . . .

There was a sharp knock on the door.

"Come in!" Harris called, coming instantly alert to the present.

The door opened and Deal Wightman entered, Eliot Trace on his heels. Of course, thought Harris wearily. Lawyers were brothers under the skin, and that was a fact. Yesterday at dinner, Harris had no doubt, both men had probably discussed what was about to happen this afternoon in the judge's chambers.

As Eliot Trace closed the door behind them, he glanced sardonically at the banker. "Surprised to see Cole Randall alive, Max?"

"Yes, damnit!" Max snapped, slumping down into his chair.

"Cole Randall is no longer a fugitive from justice."

"I know that."

Deal Wightman drifted indolently over to one of Harris's large leather armchairs against the wall and sank into it, his eyes taking note of everything. He was a thin, wraithlike person who moved like smoke at times. The features of his face were unremarkable, so pleasantly nondescript that it was difficult to gain a clear impression of the man. He had counseled Harris throughout this business, and yet Harris had never been able to gain a clear impression of what the man really thought of it all—just how far he would go to cover Harris.

Harris gave him a quick, malignant glance as he settled into the chair. Deal had certainly not given him any help in this matter. The man caught Harris's glance and shrugged, smiling slightly.

"Sorry, Max, there was really nothing I could do. Eliot didn't let a hint of what he had been planning slip out beforehand. And Judge Warner, bless the old lush, knew only that Eliot wanted to see him this afternoon on important business."

Eliot Trace sat down in the chair by Harris's desk. The man's sharp, green eyes snapped with a sullen contempt for the banker. He had taken off his hat as he sat down and now held it in his lap, his strong, bony hands holding it securely. The lawyer's thinning thatch of reddish hair gave his head a kind of angry halo. He had known and respected Del Randall since he first came to Broken Bow, had backed him in every move, taking advantage of every loophole, legal or otherwise, to smooth Randall's growing power. He had been furious, Harris knew, at the death of Del Randall.

"You'd better call off your dogs now, Max." Trace said.

"Now just what the hell do you mean by that?"

Trace looked wearily at him. "Larn was supposed to kill Cole Randall, Max, and on your orders, I have no doubt— and with Warner's warrant as a pretext. The only reason Cole is alive now is because both you and Larn thought he was dead."

"That's a damned lie!"

Trace sighed, looked at Harris for a long moment, then shook his head. "I think you should know, Max, that the trial will not be held here."

"What's that?" Deal asked, his voice betraying no alarm, the look on his face one of mild interest.

"I've already petitioned the lieutenant governor. Based on what my sources tell me, he has purchased no railroad stock recently."

"On what grounds?" Deal asked.

"The competency of our own Judge Will Warner—and

the fact that he has invested so heavily in the Northern & Central."

"And where do you plan on holding the trial?"

"Casper."

Trace looked back at Harris. "Of course, Max, I expect a lot more will come out in this trial than simply who shot U.S. Marshal Poole—with an impartial judge presiding, one who is as anxious as all of us here in Broken Bow are to get at the truth of what really happened out there—and later."

"Oh, by the way," broke in Deal casually, "Trace tells me he has sent some inquiries to Texas and Arizona Territory on Danny Larn. What he's found is interesting—and perhaps a little embarrassing."

"What he means," said Trace, "is that Danny Larn may not have that badge to hide behind much longer."

Harris looked at both men without comment. It was incredible, he thought, as a sick feeling uncoiled within his gut. Less than half an hour before, it was all in his hands. He remembered suddenly the sound of his voice booming in The Lucky Lady, announcing that the drinks were on him. In his mind's eye he saw Ross Grimsbee looking down at him through his narrow eyes, telling him that if he brought the railroad through here, all would be forgiven.

He looked at Eliot Trace. "You won't stop me. You can't. The railroad is this town's lifeblood. There are too many who know that. They won't let you stop me."

"No one wants to stop the railroad, Max," said Trace, his hard, unflinching gaze boring into Harris. "It's the way you're doing it—the price you want all of us to pay for it."

"Price?"

"The human price, Max. Everything can't be measured in dollars and cents."

Harris got to his feet. "I don't need your moralizing, Trace. It never seemed to me that you and Del Randall ever worried about the human price when a sodbuster or a small rancher came between him and what he wanted."

Eliot Trace got to his feet also, his strong, bony jaw jutting now fiercely, his eyes flashing. "I've said what I've come to say, Max. And I'll say it once again. Cole Randall is no longer a fugitive from justice, so call off your dogs."

He clapped his hat back onto his head, turned, and strode from the office. As soon as the door shut behind him, Deal Wightman got casually, almost languorously to his feet. There was a distant, reflective look in his pale eyes.

"Seems to me," the lawyer said, 'this is where I give you my last piece of advice. Keep Larn to home. Pull in your horns. Try to cut your losses. Maybe you could consider letting the Circle C and the Box W buy that land along your right of way for something approaching what Don Willard promised the ranchers."

"I need that land. I'm signing up settlers right now. This town needs those settlers."

"Maybe it don't. Maybe just keeping this high country for cattle would be a good idea. This land could still boom as a cattle country if it had that railroad to bring its beef to market."

"No."

Deal shrugged his shoulders. The man gave the impression of one who couldn't care less what Harris decided.

"Get out, Deal. You said that was your last piece of advice, so let it be just that."

The lawyer carefully set his hat back onto his head, straightened his slight shoulders just a bit and walked to the door. As he pulled it open, he looked back at Harris and seemed about to say something. But he evidently thought better of it, stepped through the door, and pulled it softly shut behind him.

Harris seethed. *Cut your losses. Pull in your horns. Keep Larn to home.* The fact that his lawyers words made good sense meant absolutely nothing to him. There was too much at stake to temporize now. He was committed. Every cent he could borrow—and yes, steal—was already sunk into this railroad. And the only way he could get his investment back was by selling first transportation, then land to those settlers. There was no way just transporting beef to market could generate enough revenue to bail him out. It was because Don Willard had been unwilling to bring in settlers—unwilling to hem the ranchers in with homesteads—that he had been unable to gain backers and had gone bankrupt.

That, Harris was convinced, was what had killed the man.

Well, it wouldn't happen to him. Indeed, the thought that Del Randall might somehow manage to reach back from beyond the grave in the person of his son and defeat him filled Harris with a black, reckless fury. He had taken care of Del Randall; he wasn't going to let his whelp ruin him. As he had known all along, Cole must die. His death was even more imperative now than it had been earlier. With Cole dead there would be no trial in Casper—and nothing left to stop Harris or the railroad. Cole's death, warrant or no warrant, was the key.

Harris thought then of Danny Larn—and of that conversation they had had in his office. The chilling lack of feeling revealed in Larn's words had unnerved him at the time. Yet this was precisely the attitude Harris realized he must now cultivate within himself. He was sowing a wind, was he? Then so be it. He would willingly reap the whirlwind as long as it took Cole Randall and the Circle C with it.

Harris got to his feet, snatched his hat up off the corner of his desk, and left his office. The bank was closing as he slipped through the door and started down the boardwalk toward the jailhouse. Larn must know by now of Cole's appearance in town, Harris realized, and was undoubtedly waiting for him. Harris smiled thinly when he recalled how angry Larn had been when Harris had refused earlier to give him the two thousand he had promised Larn for the death of Cole, insisting on Cole's body—or at least irrefutable proof of the man's death.

Well, he would increase the bounty and once again demand Cole's body. This time, he vowed grimly, he would get it.

Nine

DANNY DISMOUNTED and walked up the slight slope to the lip of the small bluff and looked across the creek at the Circle C's ranch buildings. The place was still quiet. As soon as Miles and Gil Bonney joined him, Danny leaned carefully back against a lone pine, his attention still on the compound. Then he saw a movement between the buildings and a bent old cowpoke emerged, lugging a bucket of water toward one of the horse barns.

"There goes someone," said Gil.

"Yeah," said Miles. "But that ain't Cole. An' he's been the only one on the place for the past week, him and another stove-up cowhand." Miles grabbed for his bandanna and began coughing violently into it, his eyes watering.

Gil took a careful step away from Miles. "Jesus, Miles, that goddamn cough is getting worse. You sure it ain't catchin'?"

It took a while for the spasm to subside. When it did, finally, Miles wiped his mouth carefully, his glistening eyes fastening malevolently on Gil. Gil noticed a faint spray of crimson on the man's lips before he wiped it clean. "You bet your ass it's catching, Gil," he said. "You probably got it already." He smiled. "That's what you get for opening your mouth so much."

Gil took a deep, nervous breath and looked to Danny for some comfort, but none was forthcoming from that quarter. Danny did not suffer Gil gladly. He much preferred the company of Miles; the man's sardonic view of the world matched perfectly his own. Both men were crippled and knew it and regarded the rest of mankind as beyond their pale—and beneath their contempt.

Gil Bonney had come to them on the recommendation of Fremont and Poke, both of whom were completely out of action now, with that damned Broken Bow sawbones holding out little hope that he would be able to save Fremont's leg. Gil was a sallow, pimply-faced kid with an almost leprous stench about him, the result of a seemingly pathological fear of soap and water. It was all right when the kid stayed well behind them on his horse, but when he dismounted and moved closer, or in town when he joined them at the bar, it was almost more than Danny could stand. Danny was determined that when he got this money from Harris and started back to Texas, he was not going to endure this kid's presence on the trail. He smiled inwardly at the thought. Gil and he would wash the son-of-a-bitch in a stream with a good strong yellow soap and a wire brush and then shoot him between the eyes to release him from his misery.

"Hell," said Gil, "we knowed he wasn't here. Cole Randall ain't been on this here ranch in more'n a week. So why're we spendin' our time watchin' his place for now?"

"He ain't running from that warrant," Danny said, holding in his irritation with some effort. "He might see no need to hide out now. I figured we could wait a while, see if he shows up. If he don't, we can always try the Box W. When Randall rode into town with Graham, it reminded Harris the rancher's got a daughter Randall's sweet on. So if Randall ain't here, we'll go looking for him at the Box W. You think you can remember all that, Bonney?"

Gil nodded, catching at once the casual contempt in Danny's tone. "How much did you say we'll be gettin' for this, Danny?"

Danny looked at Gil for a long minute, then turned away from the man and directed his gaze back at the Circle C spread. The old cowpoke had emerged from the barn and was heading for the ranchhouse. His legs were bowed like barrel staves and it didn't look like he'd ever make it. But he did.

Gil moved uncomfortably, aware that Danny no longer wanted to talk to him. It made him angry, but not so angry that he would protest openly. He had gotten used to having people treat him this way. He accepted it grudgingly, but he accepted it. At least these two let him stay with them.

He looked at Miles nervously and shrugged.

"Shit, man," said Miles, grimacing back a cough and reaching for his bandanna. "Don't you never listen? You and I split two thousand between us, and Danny gets three for himself."

"That's what I thought. Means Danny gets more'n twice what we get."

"That's right, Gil," said Miles. He hawked up a gob of phlegm and sent it at Gil's left boot. "Unless you ain't properly grateful—in which case all you'll get is a nice hot bullet up your ass."

At that, Danny turned quickly and looked with lidded, calculating eyes at Gil, almost as if he were measuring Gil right there for the shot.

Gil shook his head anxiously. "Now don't get me wrong," he protested. "I was just thinkin' of the other fellows, is all—seeing as how you said we might be leavin' them sudden-like. That's a fine share, sure enough. Only I just wish we could hang around and spend some of it with old Poke and Fremont—and maybe at Pauline's, too." He moistened his lips eagerly, his eyes bright at the prospect.

Miles sighed and looked at Danny. "You better tell him, Danny."

Danny glared at Gil. "We just ain't too welcome in Broken Bow, looks like. You ain't going to last much longer as a deputy and I ain't going to be wearing this here marshal's badge, neither." He glanced knowingly at Miles. "Seems like they done some checking on Miles and me."

Danny looked back then at the Circle C's ranch buildings, considering his explanation more than enough to satisfy the kid.

Gil looked at Miles. "Oh, sure, I get it. Sure thing." Gil made an effort to square his shoulders. "And I sure am glad you fellers are lettin' me in on what's going on. Don't see how I can help pull my weight, less'n I know what's really happenin'."

"Well, you been let in," said Miles. "Now shut up."

Danny turned about then and walked past them, heading back down the slope toward their horses. "Let's go," he told them. "It's getting late."

The three riders pulled up in a clump of alders after fording a stream full to overflowing with the heavy spring runoff. Dismounting, they moved carefully through the alders until they came upon a corral fence. From this vantage point they could see the ranch buildings clearly.

The Box W looked prosperous enough, Danny noted. The main house and all of its outbuildings were set on a slight elevation that commanded a view of the broad valley's sweeping grasslands and the snow-clad peaks beyond. The main house had two stories under a tiled roof and a veranda that extended the entire length of the ranchhouse.

Danny turned to Gil. "You ain't never seen this guy Graham or his daughter. That right?"

"Don't rightly recall my meetin' any of them. That's right, Danny."

"Then listen to me and do just like I say."

"I'm listening, Danny."

"Then listen, damnit!"

Gil swallowed unhappily at the rebuke and waited.

"I want you to ride across the stream and in through the gate. Hail the house, and don't dismount. You got that?"

Gil nodded anxiously.

"You tell Graham—or his daughter, if she comes out— that you're a new rider with the . . ." Danny thought a moment, trying to recall the brand of an outfit that had not thrown in with Randall. ". . . the Lazy S. You got that? The Lazy S."

"The Lady S. I got it, Danny."

"Okay. You tell them you got an important message from Ross Grimsbee. You hear that? Ross Grimsbee."

"Sure, Danny. I got it. Ross Grimsbee."

"Say the message is for Cole Randall and ask what time he's expected back. That's important, you hear? You gotta sound like you already know Randall's been staying there."

"Suppose they invite me in?"

Larn smiled then, a cold, mirthless grimace on his bone-smooth face. "I don't think they will invite you in, Gil— not if you ride close enough for them to smell you."

"Aw, hell, Danny . . . !"

"But if they do, that'll mean either Cole's in there or he's expected back soon. Either way, you go on inside and wait till we join you. If they don't invite you in or tell you when Cole's coming back, it's more than likely Cole ain't holing up there, after all. So you just thank them and ride off. You got all that?"

For a moment Gil seemed puzzled; then he brightened. "Oh, sure. I got you, Danny. If Cole ain't holin' up there, they most likely won't invite me in, so if they do that means he's there or comin' by soon, so go right on in and stall until you guys show up.

"You catch on just fine," Danny said. He reached out and slapped Gil on the back to puff him up a little. "Just fine. Now get on your horse and do it just like I said. Miles and me'll be right here, watching the whole thing."

Gil left them and disappeared beyond the trees. A moment later they heard the soft thud of his horse's hooves on the grassy sward and then the sound of the horse and rider splashing into the swift stream. In about ten minutes Gil appeared just beyond the gate, riding toward it.

"I hope that asshole don't forget what I told him."

"He smells pretty bad, Danny, but he ain't all that dumb."

Danny shook his head. "That's hard to believe, Miles."

They were silent then as they watched Gil ride up to the ranchhouse. They saw him pull up and then heard his faint voice as he hailed the house. A moment later, the door to the ranchhouse opened and a slight woman, not more than twenty it seemed to Danny, stepped out onto the veranda. She had on an apron and shading her eyes against the low sun she peered up at Gil as he spoke to her.

"She's the only one there, most likely," Danny said.

Gil finished talking. The woman began replying to Gil. There was something in the lift of her head that told Danny what he needed to know. Cole was staying there, all right, and she was inviting Gil in to wait for him.

Even as he thought this, he saw Gil dismount. The woman said a few words to him, pointing to the horse barn as she did. Gil nodded and led his horse toward the barn.

Danny grinned at Miles. "Maybe she's going to make the filthy son-of-a-bitch wait in there with the other animals."

Miles chuckled.

A few moments later Gil left the horse barn and started for the ranchhouse.

"That settles it. If Cole ain't in there, he sure as hell is on his way. Wait until Gil gets inside, then we'll make our move."

Miles nodded, withdrew his six-gun from its holster, and spun the cylinder. Then he holstered it and grinned at Danny. "Shall we leave our horses here?"

"For now. Once we get control of the place, we can stash them in the barn so Randall won't notice anything when he rides in. But we better hurry it up. It's getting toward sundown. He might be due back soon."

Miles nodded and the two men left the cover of the alders, slipped through the corral fences, then darted across the compound to the house. When Danny reached the veranda, he slowed abruptly and looked around to see if any hands were coming out of any of the outbuildings or riding in from the grasslands back of the ranchhouse. But he saw and heard no one. He mounted the veranda, stepping as lightly as possible, and approached one of the windows. Looking in, he glimpsed Gil sitting at the kitchen table with his back to the window, watching the girl fuss with a pot on the stove. He ducked past the window. Reaching the door, he unholstered one of his Smith & Wessons and with his left hand turned the doorknob—and pushed. The door swung wide and Danny stepped into a large hall, Miles at his heels. There was a broad staircase in front of him, an open door to his right leading into the kitchen.

"Who's there?" he heard the girl cry.

The two men strode swiftly into the kitchen. Danny trained his weapon on the girl. Her surprise became fury when she saw Danny.

"What are you doing in my kitchen?" she demanded. "Get out of here! Both of you!"

Gil was already on his feet. "Cole Randall's coming, all

right," he told Danny. "She mentioned that she didn't expect him to be too late. Said he rode over to the Double Bar."

"That's that outfit in the Sawtooths," said Miles. "Them's the bastards got us before on that ridge."

Gil nodded eagerly. "Maybe we ought to get them before we clear out."

"Shut up," said Danny. "Who the hell put you in charge?" He looked back at Miles. "Cole won't be here before dark then," he said thoughtfully. "So, we'll just wait, let him walk right into our parlor." He looked over at Gil. "Who else is around? Did she say?"

Gil smiled proudly. "Her father and his hired hand should be in soon for supper, she told me. They're off rounding up some strays."

"Oh! You!" the girl cried, looking at Gil. She was furious at him—and at herself for talking so much, Danny realized.

"Maybe that's them now," said Miles.

Danny listened and heard the clop of hoofs and the sound of two men talking casually above them. Danny stepped quickly to the window and looked out. He saw Bill Graham swing out of his saddle and a cowhand already leading his horse, both men headed for the barn.

"We'll just sit tight and wait for them," said Danny.

"No you won't!" cried the girl as she darted for the kitchen door leading directly outside.

"Grab her!" said Danny.

Both Miles and Gil rushed for her, but it was Gil who caught up to her in the open doorway and pulled her back into the kitchen. She tried to scream out, but she managed only a single, strange strangled sound as Miles clapped his hand over her mouth. She began to twist wildly then, beating at them futilely with her tiny, ineffectual hands. Both Gil and Miles had a difficult time holding her. Twice she clawed Miles's hand from her mouth and managed an abortive cry. Gil looked across the room to Danny for help.

"Hit her!" Danny told Gil. "Shut her up good. They're coming out of the barn now."

"I can't." He yelped suddenly as the girl managed to kick him viciously in the shins.

Now she was twisting out of Miles's grasp, clawing for the door. "Fools!" Danny cried angrily.

In four swift strides he was beside the girl. He grabbed her hair and yanked her backward with such fury that she lost her footing and slammed violently onto the kitchen floor. When the small of her back hit, she let out a tiny cry of surprise, then started to roll over, sobbing hysterically. Danny stepped back, then kicked her on the point of her jaw. Her head swiveled violently, her body seemed to twitch convulsively, then she lay still.

"Check the window," Danny told Miles, as he knelt to examine the girl.

He felt her pulse. It was beating regularly. Carefully, he took her jaw in his hand and moved it from side to side. Satisfied it was not broken and that the girl was only unconscious, he straightened up and looked across the kitchen at Miles.

"They're coming in by the side kitchen door," Miles told him.

"Okay. Both of us cover the door." Danny made no effort to move or hide in any way the girl's body. "Gil, get over near the wall. As soon as they step inside, you get between them and the door."

Gil nodded and hurried to flatten himself against the wall. The door was pulled open. Graham stepped into the kitchen first, saw his daughter sprawled on the floor, and let out a startled cry. Behind him, the cowhand asked what was wrong and pushed past him. In the next instant, both men were staring at the drawn guns of Miles and Danny.

"What have you done with my daughter!" Graham called, rushing to the girl's side and kneeling by her.

As the cowhand followed the man into the kitchen, Gil moved behind him and slammed shut the door. The cowhand stopped in his tracks and slowly raised his hands.

"That's fine," said Danny. "You just keep them up like that, cowboy." Then he looked down at Graham. "She'll be all right. She got kind of hysterical and I had to quiet her."

The man sprang to his feet, beside himself with fury. "We'll get you for this! We'll follow you to the gates of hell! You've gone too far now, Larn!"

Danny looked at Graham and smiled thinly. "Maybe."

Graham dropped back beside the girl. Gently he lifted her head and shoulders, then rested the back of her head in the crook of his arm. Carefully he felt her bruised, already swollen face. Almost enviously, Danny watched the tears coursing unashamedly down the man's face.

Miles stepped closer and looked down at the girl. "If we kill her, Danny, there ain't going to be a state or territory we'll be safe in. Maybe we better go a bit easy on her."

"She'll have a sore jaw for a while, that's all."

Miles shrugged and went over to a kitchen chair and slumped into it. He began to cough then, the sound of his tearing lungs filling the kitchen.

Danny looked at Gil. "Go get our horses and stable them. Grain them but leave the saddles on. And bring back some rope or rawhide. We got a long wait for Randall, looks like, and it'll be a lot more restful if we truss up these jaspers and stuff a sock or something into their mouths."

Gil nodded and hurried out the kitchen door.

Still cradling his daughter's head, Graham looked up at Danny. "There's no warrant out on Cole now. He's free on bail. You're planning to murder him, aren't you?"

Danny looked for a moment down at Graham without answering, then glanced over at the cowhand, who was still standing in front of the table with his hands up. "Unbuckle your gunbelt," he told the man, "and let it drop."

He glanced then at Miles, who got up wearily. As the cowhand's belt dropped to the floor, Miles bent and picked it up. Danny then waggled his revolver at Graham. "Come on, Graham. Undo that belt."

Seething inwardly, Graham let his daughter's head down gently onto the floor, then stood up slowly. Danny watched the man's eyes. They were wild with rage. The man's hands dropped to his belt buckle. He made a half-hearted move to release it; then his hand flew to his holster. With a grin, Miles stepped close and brought the barrel of his six-gun down on the side of the rancher's head. He went down heavily, landing just beside his daughter. Danny swung his revolver toward the cowhand.

The fellow had taken an angry step toward Miles. He pulled up quickly, however, when he saw the gun pointed at his gut.

"You bastards," he said softly.

Danny cocked his Smith & Wesson and toyed momentarily with the idea of sending a bullet into the man below the belt line. The cowhand's face went pale.

"Beg, cowhand."

"Like I said," the fellow replied, his voice ragged. "You're a bastard. Pull the trigger, if you want. I don't beg to turds like you."

Danny nodded, satisfied, and holstered his weapon. "Get over there by the stove and hunker down on the floor. Keep your hands where I can see them."

As the cowhand did as Danny directed, Danny looked back at the girl and her father. The two of them—along with the cowhand—would be witnesses to the killing of Randall. It was never a good idea to leave anyone behind that could testify. That was how he had lived so long on this side of a jailhouse window. He would have to kill them all. And he would have to make it look like an accident.

A fire should take care of things nicely, he concluded finally. When Miles saw the logic of it, he wouldn't fuss. It wouldn't matter if he did.

"Miles," Danny said, "collect all the kerosene lamps and bring them in here."

Miles had been in the act of letting himself down into the kitchen chair again. He straightened wearily and looked at Danny, a frown on his face. Then he looked about him at the girl and her father and at the cowhand sitting on the floor against the wall.

"Hell, Danny."

"'You want witnesses?"

Miles thought a moment, then shrugged and left the kitchen in search of kerosene lanterns.

Cole galloped up alongside Nancy and reined in. She did likewise. Both let their horses blow some as they watched Blue and Ryan disappearing into the draw at an easy lope. When they were out of sight, Cole looked at Nancy.

"This gather should do it then. How many head would you say?"

"Close to thirty. Blue found them. They'd wintered near Indian Spring. They're spindly, Blue says, but they made it through all right." She smiled. "This valley grass will fatten them real quick, Cole. Help with the calvin' too, I'm thinking."

Cole nodded. "It should."

"You mean what you said, Cole—the Double Bar and the Circle C are partners?"

"Why not? There's plenty of graze in this valley and the hills around for Circle C and Double Bar—for all of us. That's what we'll settle with the Box W tonight. Bill Graham's a stubborn ol' cuss—a lot like my father was, but he'll come around."

"You certainly don't sound like your father, Cole."

He looked at her, considering her words and his response. He supposed she was right, at that. A pair of antic yellow butterflies fluttered about Nancy's hat for a moment. "No one's exactly like anyone else, Nancy. There's a lot of my father in me, I'm sure. But there's others somewhere inside too, sure enough. And then there's me—what I make of it all, I reckon."

"Your mother, Cole. Do you remember much about her?"

"She was gone even before I could ride, Nancy. I guess Consuelo was my mother."

"And she's gone."

"Back to her people." Cole frowned. "Like her job was done with my father gone. Didn't even say good-bye."

"Did she need to?"

He frowned thoughtfully, surprised at Nancy's insight. "Guess not. Now that I think of it, we did talk some after the funeral." He smiled. "She was never much for long conversations."

"Neither are you, Cole."

He nodded soberly. "What about you, Nancy? How much like your mother are you?"

She laughed outright, then sobered. "Not much, I'll admit. Not much at all—at least in the way she took things."

"Oh?"

"'I watched my ma work herself to a nubbin on a Nebraska farm,'" Nancy said with sudden intensity. "Her hands were raw and cracked from home-boiled soap, her face pinched. She was always flinching from the dust, the wind, the damned, never-ending toil. Pa and the rest of us, we rode out and did things, while she stayed behind in that mean little sod house and worked. I think, finally, it was the dust that killed her. It sifted from the walls and the roof that pa was always going to fix with planking." Nancy

143

stopped talking then and looked away from Cole.

Cole waited, aware that his question had stirred to life a long-smoldering memory.

Nancy looked back at Cole. "You see, it never did any good to clean anything. Mud in the spring. Dust in the summer. And soot all winter from the wood stove. And no room for anything. She just gave up, I guess. The dirt, the toil, the emptiness of the land and the sky overhead, it was all too much for her."

Cole nodded, knowing at once what Nancy meant. Even out here, in land not half so demanding, he had heard of women who had been unable to stand the loneliness and unrelenting work of life on an isolated ranch. He wondered if that wasn't part of what had killed his own mother.

"She died gratefully, Cole," Nancy continued, her voice soft, musing. "I remember what she told me just before she died."

"What was that?"

"Don't do it, she told me. And when I asked her what she meant, she said *This! Don't do this! Away! Get away! Don't do—any of it!* A few hours later she was dead. And you know what, Cole? I haven't done any of it and I won't."

Cole smiled. "Not even if the right man came along?"

"Not on your life, Cole. No one is right enough to turn a woman into something like that."

"I see."

Nancy looked at him shrewdly, the trace of a smile on her face. "Don't you worry, Cole. You've got someone waiting for you now. From what I can gather, all she wants is to settle down with you and be chief cook and bottle washer. And the mother of your children."

She meant Linda, he realized. And of course Nancy was right. That was all Linda wanted, and she was anxiously waiting now for him to set the date. They had grown surprisingly close this past week while she tended him. Her patience with him was incredible and her love—well, it made him feel strangely unworthy. Unfit even. No man—certainly not he—deserved that kind of unreserved, uncritical devotion. He shifted uneasily in his saddle at the memory of it.

"She loves you, Cole. Very much."

"I know she does."

"Be grateful then."

"You mean don't look a gift horse in the mouth."

"I guess that's what I mean."

Cole nodded, but remained still somewhat disquieted by the prospect of marriage. What was the matter with him, he wondered irritably. This girl sitting her horse beside him felt nothing for him. Further, he had known her for only a few weeks. She was more like a man than a woman and for that reason he owed his life to her. Hell, she rode a horse better than most men and could outshoot just as many. She wasn't really a woman at all—not, certainly, in the way Linda was.

And yet, despite all this, his thoughts about her . . .

The sound of brawling critters broke into his thoughts. Nancy pulled her mount and quickly lifted her horse to a gallop as she headed for the draw. Cole rode after her and was pulling up beside her when the Double Bar cattle—gaunt from the long winter in the high country—spilled out of the draw, blatting happily at sight of lush grassland.

As Ryan and Blue drove them from behind, Nancy and Cole kept them in a line until they crossed the flat, then turned them into a lowland meadow bordered by one of the mountain-fed streams that flowed into the valley. It would be only a trickle this summer when most of the snow fields had melted, but right now it was running full, overflowing its banks in spots.

"This'll be just fine," said Nancy, smiling in appreciation. She turned in her saddle to greet her brothers riding up. "Looks like closer to forty head here!"

Blue grinned as he pulled up alongside them. Looking

straight at Cole, he said, "Found some unbranded stock in a ravine. Mavericks. Guess we'll just have to split 'em with Circle C."

Cole laughed. They were obviously Circle C cattle this far down. "Right generous of you, Blue. Thank you."

Both men laughed, Nancy right along with them.

"'How long do you reckon it'll take for us to ride to the Box W?" Blue asked. "It's getting on to dusk already."

"We can make it in a couple of hours, seems to me. We don't have to push it. Linda will have something hot for us. I told her I was bringing you, and she's right anxious to see you again, Nancy."

Nancy smiled. "Let's go then."

As they rode off together, Cole found himself riding alongside Blue with Nancy pulling up behind them alongside Ryan. He felt better at once and chided himself for what he now considered his disloyal thoughts concerning Linda.

A man had to choose the sensible course, not let himself be carried away on impulse like some child who didn't know the difference between his wants and his needs.

Ten

LINDA COULD hear Larn instructing the youngest of the two men with him to take Cy out to the bunkhouse. The fellow Larn called Gil was to tie Cy up and then wait for Cole to show up. Gil was not to open fire until Cole did, and Larn was going to wait until Cole had dismounted in front of the ranchhouse or barn.

Larn did not know what Linda knew: that Cole would not be alone, that he was planning on bringing the Doblers with him. But that didn't matter, Linda thought despairingly. Danny Larn would kill all of them.

She heard Cy and Gil leaving the kitchen. Opening her eyes just a crack, she saw the look of desperation on old Cy's face and hoped he didn't try anything foolish. The one called Gil had an unstable cockiness about him that frightened her. He would do anything, she sensed, to prove himself to the others. Cy and the deputy disappeared out the door.

She closed her eyes and listened to the sounds of the others remaining in the kitchen behind her. Her father—his hands also tied behind him—had been thrown down beside her against the wall. He was only partially conscious and every once in a while would groan softly. She did not know what they had done to him, but he was obviously in great pain. For the last half hour or so she had been working on the rope they had wound about her wrists. Her wrists were small. She had been making bread when Larn broke in, and there was still flour and some lard on her hands and wrists when they tied her.

One hand was almost free, her left. She tugged, felt the rough rope tearing through the already raw skin. Then she was loose. She flexed her fingers and gradually restored the circulation in her hand. The pins-and-needles sting that flooded through the hand as the circulation returned almost caused her to cry out, it was so intense. She kept her hand behind her back and opened her eyes slightly to look around. They hadn't noticed anything. Larn's deputy was at the table. Danny Larn was standing beside the window, peering out into the night.

She closed her eyes again and with her free hand pulled the loose rope off her right wrist, then waited for the circulation in that hand to return also. When it had, she slowly reached down to her legs and began to loosen the rope they had wrapped around her ankles.

This movement caught the eye of Larn's deputy. He had been coughing dryly, wearily into a filthy bandanna. Getting to his feet, he walked slowly over and stood looking down at her. Her eyes open now, her mouth agonizingly dry with the piece of tablecloth they had stuffed into it, she began to struggle, as if she were still securely bound and wanted only to be let loose.

The man looked back across the kitchen at Danny Larn. "Hey, you think maybe we should loosen this girl's rope some?"

Larn looked at Linda, his eyes cold, unfeeling. "No, and make sure that cloth we got stuffed in her mouth is secure. We don't want her letting out any last-minute yells."

The fellow nodded negligently and reached down, grabbed a tuft of the cloth that was protruding from her mouth and shoved it in deeper. Linda gasped deep in her throat and fell back, tears flooding her eyes, ruining her vision of the man. She saw him smile, then turn and walk back to the table and the coffee he was sipping.

She blinked away the tears and reached once more for her ankles, struggling fitfully all the while. As she worked on the rope around her ankles, the deputy occasionally glanced over at her. But he paid no attention to her movements now. After what seemed to her an eternity, she had loosened the ropes sufficiently to enable her to flex her ankles. If she wanted to do so, she knew, she could kick loose the rope and stand up now and perhaps make a rush for one of them.

But she did not want to do this now. Not until Cole came. Then her action would warn him away, save him. For they would easily overpower her now and then be free to let Cole enter their trap without hindrance. No. She must wait until Cole was close enough to be warned by what he heard coming from this kitchen. She lay back, her head resting against the wainscoting.

This movement of hers caused her father's head to change position and she saw that his eyes were open, staring at her.

Thank God! she thought. He had regained consciousness!

She winked slowly at him and he returned the wink, but weakly, as if it took enormous concentration to get the job done. This fact troubled her, but did not entirely discourage her. At least he was conscious and able to communicate that fact to her.

She measured the passage of time by the cups of coffee the deputy at the table drank. She could not see out the window, but she knew there was to be a nearly full moon this night, and that meant that Cole would be clearly visible as he and the Doblers rode into the compound.

She could not let them get that far then.

It was when the dryness in her mouth from the tablecloth reached an almost unbearable level and she was tempted to throw all caution to the winds and rip the thing from her mouth that she heard Danny bark softly to his deputy.

"There's a rider coming—out there byond the gate."

The deputy got up from his chair and walked over to the window. Both men kept to the side of the window so that their shadows would not warn the oncoming riders. As this second one peered out into the moonlit night, Danny Larn swore softly.

"He ain't alone! There's three other riders with him!"

The deputy smiled wolfishly at Danny Larn. "Hell, Danny, that makes it almost even, don't it."

"Surprise'll make it even," said Danny Larn coldly. "Wonder who the hell they are."

Larn glanced quickly over at Linda, then hurried across the kitchen to her. Going down on one knee beside her, he unholstered his gleaming six-gun and cocked it, resting the muzzle firmly against Linda's temple. Then he took the gag out of her mouth.

"You knew Cole Randall was coming back with some-one," he said. "Who are they?"

Linda compressed her lips tightly.

Larn slapped her hard, so hard that it brought tears to her eyes and caused her mouth to fly open.

"I'll ask you once more," he said, pressing the muzzle

of the revolver painfully into her temple.

Linda calculated swiftly. Larn had said that the riders were outside the gate. And that was only moments before. They were still riding closer and already they were close enough for Larn to have been able to pick out individual riders. In only a few seconds more they would have ridden in through the gate. That meant they were close enough!

"I . . . I don't know," she said, stalling, knowing it would anger Larn further.

But Larn did not pull the trigger. Instead, he slapped her a second time, driving her head back against the wall. For a second she thought she would lose consciousness. Then she heard the other one's voice.

"They're coming on," he said.

Larn turned his head to reply to the deputy. Linda pushed herself away from the wall and grabbed at the man's neck with both hands, flattening him with the fury of her attack. She was on top of him then, raking his face with her fingers. He tried to scramble away, but she was like a wildcat and began screaming as she tore at his face and neck.

Larn still had his gun. He brought it up and tried to shoot her in his panic. The gun fired, its powerful detonation causing the walls of the kitchen to vibrate like a drum. The bullet missed, however, and smashed into the shattered remnants of a kerosene lamp that had been hurled to the floor earlier.

With a soft *whump* the kerosene-saturated floor exploded into flame. Cursing wildly at Linda, Larn rolled away from her, brought up his gun a second time, and fired into her. Linda felt the impact of the slug as a violent punch in her midsection that sent her stumbling back against the wall. There was surprisingly little pain, and she scrambled to her feet and ran forward toward the window.

"Cole!" she cried. "Cole! Get away! It's Larn! Get away!"

The deputy swung his revolver and caught her on the

side of the face with the barrel. The force of the blow knocked her spinning into the now blazing corner of the room. She heard as well as felt the roar of the flames as they enveloped her. A searing tongue of fire lanced up her right thigh. She tried to beat the flame away and saw that the entire hem of her long dress was afire. Then her hair seemed to come alive and she realized it too was aflame.

By this time her wound caused her to lose what little strength she had left to fight the flames. Every inhalation was searing her lungs and an excruciating crown of pain was crushing down upon her skull. She beat feebly at the flames sweeping up from her skirt, then sank onto the seething floor and began to scream. She screamed over and over until the screaming seemed to be coming from someone else.

And then it faded. She felt suddenly alone and thought of Cole with an aching sense of loss, then tried to wrap her arms about herself for comfort. But she had no arms. She had nothing—only pain. . . .

At the sound of the shot, Cole pulled up, alarmed.

"Something's wrong here," he told Blue tensely.

And then came the second shot from within the ranchhouse. A third spat at him from the bunkhouse. The slug whispered over his right shoulder. But it was the ranchhouse Cole was watching. The first shots had undoubtedly come from there. He noticed suddenly the growth in intensity of the light behind the kitchen window.

"The kitchen's on fire!" Nancy said.

Then Cole heard Linda calling his name. Like a voice from another world—it came to him through the walls of the ranchhouse, faint but clear across the still, moonlit compound.

"*. . . Cole! Get away! It's Larn! Get away!*"

As another shot came at them from the bunkhouse, Cole pulled his horse around and raced back out through the gate, the others following. It was a trap! Larn and his deputies—how many Cole had no idea—had been waiting in that kitchen and bunkhouse for them to dismount and walk into their guns.

Since Cole was no longer a legal prize, there was no doubt in Cole's mind what Larn intended. All pretense of following the law was being abandoned by Maxwell Harris. Get Cole Randall. It didn't matter how. Just get him.

Danny Larn winced slightly at the girl's screams, but made no effort to help her or her father still bound on the floor as he ran for the kitchen door. The growing heat leaned on his back like a heavy hand. He flung open the door and ran out, Miles right behind him. Opening the door had acted like a bellows on the flames and they pumped suddenly throughout the house, illuminating the ground before the two running men almost as brightly as if it were full daylight.

As Larn headed for the bunkhouse, he called over his shoulder to Miles, "Get the horses ready!"

Miles nodded and darted for the barn as Danny pushed open the bunkhouse door. The burning ranchhouse sent yellow bands of light streaming through the bunkhouse windows. Gil Bonney's upper torso was brightly visible, his head and shoulders in complete darkness. Behind him, the trussed ranchhand was sitting on the floor between two bunks, his back against the wall. A bandanna had been knotted around his head by Gil, covering his mouth completely. The man was alert. In the dim light between the bunks, the whites of his eyes were clearly visible to Danny.

At Danny's entrance Gil, who had been crouching at the window with his six-gun, got to his feet. "I fired soon's I heard you shootin' from the ranchhouse, Danny. What happened? We should've waited."

"Never mind that. Kill this one and let's go."

"Kill him?" Gil swallowed and stepped back from the

window so that his entire face was caught in the livid glow from the burning ranchhouse. "Jesus, Danny!"

Danny unholstered his Smith & Wesson. In the dancing light it gleamed brightly and Gil eyed it with sudden fear. And well he might, thought Danny furiously. "Get out there," he told him. "I'll take care of this one then." He smiled at the look of pure relief that flooded Gil's face. "And then you can keep right on going home to mama."

Gil did not respond to Danny's gibe; he was in too much of a hurry to get out of the bunkhouse. As he disappeared out the door, Danny turned his attention to the ranchhand. He sighted carefully on the man's chest, aiming at a point slightly to the right of his solar plexus, and fired. He did not see the bullet penetrate the man's vest, but he saw the fellow slam back still tighter against the wall. Yet he remained upright and still seemed to be looking at him. Danny aimed quickly and fired a second time, this bullet planting a neat hole in the ranchhand's forehead just above his left eye. As the hole grew slowly larger, the man's eyes appeared to grow wider as well, their gaze seeming to penetrate deep into Danny's soul.

Danny stood there for a moment, irresolute, debating foolishly whether or not he should send still another bullet into the dead man when the sound of hoofs approaching the open bunkhouse aroused him. He holstered his weapon and left the place.

The light from the blazing ranchhouse reached out now to encompass the entire ranch compound. Even the grass around corral posts and along the boardwalk leading from the bunkhouse to the barn was glowing an unnaturally lush green. He grabbed the reins that Miles threw him and vaulted into his saddle. Clapping spurs to his horse, he led the way from the compound, glad suddenly to put behind him that furious, hellish glow. . . .

Well into the flat beyond the gate, Cole pulled up. As he looked back, the ranchhouse exploded into flames. In the unnatural glow of the fire, he saw two figures rush from the house, one heading for the barn, the other for the bunkhouse. As he pulled his horse around completely, he saw a rider leading two horses across the compound to the bunkhouse.

In that awful moment Cole realized the full extent of the horror Danny Larn had loosed on him. *Linda was still in that inferno! Her father too—and Cy!*

"Back! Go back!" he cried to Blue and Ryan. "Linda's in that fire!"

As they galloped back across the flat, three riders broke from the compound and disappeared behind the ranchhouse, heading for the dim mass of foothills that crouched in the night south of the Box W. If Larn and his men reached those hills before this night was out, Cole realized, they would be long gone.

But that didn't matter. Not right now it didn't. Cole clattered in through the gate and galloping up to the crackling ranchhouse flung himself from his horse. Shielding his face with his arms, he bolted up onto the veranda.

Someone flung himself at him from the side, caught him about the knees, and drove him off the low porch to the ground. Cole struggled to free himself and felt another pair of arms grab him from behind. It was Blue who had tackled him first and now Ryan held him.

"Let me go!" he cried. "Let me go!"

"It's too late!" Blue yelled at him, above the roar of the fire. "You wouldn't last in there a second! It's no use!"

And then Nancy was beside him. "Be sensible, Cole! Nothing could live in that!"

Cole slumped weakly, aware that his head was throbbing sickeningly. Ryan let him go. Cole stood dazed, feeling his eyebrows burning, his eyes growing raw as the heat dried them out. He squinted and took a few steps back. The others moved back with him. The fire had spread throughout the ranchhouse now, growing gluttonous as it roared up into the second story and began licking hungrily at the roof.

Cole turned his back on the fire and led his horse away. The flames had made the animal skittish and it had to be gentled. Cole patted its neck absently, fighting back the sobs of rage and loss that threatened to erupt within him. He heard the booming now of the roof beams cracking in the heat, and rested his forehead upon the cantle and hung on.

As Danny crested a low rise and looked back, he saw the night horizon still bright with the glow from the fire and allowed himself a smile.

"We better make tracks, huh, Danny?" Gil said, glancing uneasily at him. The kid still was not sure what Danny intended to do to him for refusing to shoot the ranchhand, and Danny enjoyed letting the kid worry about it.

"What's the matter, Gil? You so damned anxious to run home to mama?"

"Aw, now listen, Danny . . . !"

"What are you going to do, Gil—shoot me? Go ahead, why don't you. Teach me a lesson."

Gil looked away from Danny, his thin face pinched with rage. For a moment Danny wished the kid would go for his iron, but he knew the punk had long since lost the guts for it.

Miles finished coughing into his bandanna. Through red-rimmed eyes, he looked at Danny. The man seemed enormously weary as he clung to his saddle horn and let his emaciated form lean over the cantle. "He's right, you know, Danny. We damn well better keep on going south until we get into them hills. We left a dead girl back there—and her father too."

"We left dead bodies, all right. But we left no witnesses. Cole Randall and them with him heard shots. They was warned and rode out of the place. When they came back, they found three dead bodies—and nothing solid to use against us, nothing they could take into a court of law that would sure as hell prove we was the ones that did it."

Miles shrugged. "Sure, but . . . well, hell, Danny, everyone knows we're after Cole Randall."

"Sure. Cole Randall. But not the Grahams. Not Box W."

"What do we do then?"

"I been thinking on that. We still got our badges on our vests—and a judge in our back pocket. No need for us to run anywhere—even if we do lose our badges sometime tomorrow. We'll have them long enough, I'm thinking."

"You mean we're goin' back to Broken Bow?" Gil asked, shocked.

"We would've had to go back anyways for the payoff if we got Randall. Only difference from now is we would've sneaked in tonight and made it out by daybreak." Danny smiled. "Sure, we'll go back. If Harris was willing to part with all that cash to see Cole Randall dead, how much do you think the son-of-a-bitch'll pay now—to save his goddamn hide?"

Gil frowned in obvious befuddlement, but Miles saw the point at once, his emaciated face twisting into an ironic, appreciative smile.

Danny slapped the rump of his mount with his reins and led them in a sudden gallop off the rise. Keeping the red glow in the skies to his left, he set his course for Broken Bow. Miles had seen it just as he did. Randall would come for him and Harris, and when he did, Danny would be waiting.

Only this time he would be sure to get the money first—all of it.

Eleven

MAXWELL HARRIS came awake quickly and glanced out the window of his hotel room. The sun had not yet risen, though the eastern sky was lightening. It was not the coming dawn that had awakened him, but the sound of shod hooves on the street below. Having slept fitfully, this had been enough to arouse him and now he threw back his quilted coverlet and padded on bare feet to the window and looked down.

Danny Larn and two of his deputies, the consumptive and that hatchet-faced kid, were riding past the hotel. As Harris watched, Larn rode up the street and turned his horse in at the hitch rail in front of his office, while the other two continued on down the street to the saloon loft where they had been staying. Larn said something to the men as they rode on, then turned and entered his office.

As soon as the door closed behind him, Harris moved

159

back from the window and slumped down on the bed. A desolate sense that something had gone wrong—terribly wrong—had fallen over him the moment he saw those three men riding past the hotel. And yet, there was no earthly reason why he should feel this way. Danny Larn was the coldest, most ruthless killer he had ever known. If he had gone after Cole Randall with those two, he must have succeeded in killing Cole and was now back in town to collect his bounty.

Of course. It was as simple as that. And all Harris had to do now was dress and deal with the man—give him his money, then bid him good riddance. Harris tried to accustom himself to thinking of Cole Randall dead. It was going to bring inquiries, of course, but no more than were already coming his way. The difference was that with Cole gone, there'd be no trial, no finger pointing at him any longer. In a few months, with Danny Larn and his gunslingers long gone, the talk would quiet down, the train whistle would be heard in the land, and the only thing the townsmen and the cattlemen who hadn't tried to stop him would remember was that he was the man who turned the trick—turned Broken Bow into a thriving metropolis up here in the high country.

Harris had gone over this scenario in his mind many times in the past hours, ever since he had dispatched Danny Larn on his grisly errand—and each time it had never failed to bolster his spirits and send his shoulders back. But now, in the dim, gray light of a new day, this bracing vision of what must come failed to dispel the uneasiness that was growing on him with each passing second.

He took a deep breath and looked around him. His was the only apartment in the hotel. Three rooms comprised the suite, and all were roomy indeed, by Western standards. He had a living room, a large interior room where he took his meals, and this bedroom. There was not an item of furniture that was not the very best. An imported oriental covered the living room, and the rest of the carpeting and the few scatter rugs were thick and luxurious underfoot. He had a cleaning woman come in every day to keep the place spotless. Not a chair or a table was out of place, not a lamp that did not gleam, not a surface that was not polished. And yet, as Harris looked around him at his immaculate suite, all he felt was a bitter, sterile loneliness.

He stood up and shrugged into his robe, found the slippers and pushed his feet into them, then walked over to the wash stand and poured the water into the wash bowl. He stood, looking unhappily down at the tepid water, and decided he would not shave. His hands, he knew, were too unsteady at this moment. The trouble, he realized, was that he was handling all this alone, that these enormous decisions he had been facing up to over these past months had been made without the advice—or comfort—of a loved one, someone to whom he could unburden himself.

A wife, perhaps.

He thought of Mary then—and that led to thoughts of Delmar Randall. The old anger kindled his spirits nicely, made him shake off his somber mood of self-pity. It was strange. He had killed Delmar Randall—had actually shot the man down, swept him off his saddle with a blast from his shotgun—and yet the man haunted him yet, still seemed to be hovering about to remind Harris of how futile he was—of how little he had after all, compared to all that Del Randall had once had. . . .

Mary! Oh, Jesus! Why did you marry him?

He turned from the wash stand and hurried to the closet to dress. He would face Larn unshaven. He would pay the man and be rid of him—and of the ghost, finally, of Delmar Randall.

Perhaps it would rid him of Mary's ghost as well.

The sun was brightening the tops of the false fronts when Harris stepped into Larn's office. He saw the man with his back to him, bare to the waist, carefully sponging away the sweat and grime of his long ride. Larn turned at Harris's entrance and nodded, the tiniest flicker of a smile on his skull-like face. He needed a shave, Harris noted, reminding himself as he did that he had never seen Danny Larn in public without his pale, tightly drawn skin immaculately clean-shaven.

As Harris settled into the chair by Larn's desk, Larn turned back to his morning toilet without comment. Harris waited impatiently for the man to speak. When Larn finished sponging off his torso and reached for his straight razor, Harris lost his patience completely.

"Well?" he demanded.

Again Larn turned to face him, his razor held in his right hand. With a sardonic smile, he lifted his chin and began to shave. "Wait, Harris," he said between strokes. "It's a long story."

"Is he dead?"

Larn turned his back on Harris and bent so that he could see his reflection in the small mirror he had propped against the wash bowl. With infinite care, he wielded the razor. The sound of the blade scraping off Larn's beard filled the room. "No," he said, shifting his position slightly to give himself a better view of the left side of his face. "He got away."

Oh, God! Harris thought. *It's not over yet!*

Larn was using the straight razor with great skill as he shaved about his pencil thin mustache. Watching him, Harris thought he would jump up at any minute and rip the blade from the son-of-a-bitch's hand. But he ground his teeth and forced himself to wait.

As Larn straightened and dipped the razor into the wash basin to clean it off, Harris said tightly, "What do you mean, it's a long story? What happened?"

Turning to face him, Larn wiped his face dry with a towel, then pulled the long blade through it. He smiled as he walked over to an open trunk sitting in a chair on the far side of the room. "You won't like it," he said, reaching into his trunk for a clean silk shirt. "You won't like it one bit. But it was the best we could do."

As he said this last, his eyes regarded Harris with a kind of pleased malice.

"What the hell do you mean, damnit? Speak up, man! What happened?"

"We set up a trap for Cole in the Box W. But the girl . . ."

"Linda Graham?"

"That's her, I guess. Well, she caused a rumpus and warned Cole off."

Harris caught something in Larn's explanation, something hidden just beneath the surface that tickled Larn immensely. The man wasn't telling all of it because he savored it and wanted to enjoy it slowly, like a little boy with a piece of store candy.

And then Harris got a faint glimmer of what it was that Danny Larn was savoring—and that he knew Harris would not like. "The Grahams," he said. "What about them? You didn't . . ."

"Like I said," Larn replied, buttoning his shirt carefully, "the girl set up a rumpus to warn Cole Randall. There was some shooting and the place went up in flames."

"Oh, my God," Harris groaned. "Bill Graham—and Linda!"

"And their hired hand."

"Cy Reese."

"That's right. The three of them."

"You mean all of them . . . were burned to death in the fire?" Harris could not believe what he was hearing.

"Not all of them. I had to shoot Reese."

Harris looked at Larn for a long moment. "You *had* to shoot him?" he asked stupidly, aware that Larn was regarding him with a cold, detached amusement.

"That's right. Didn't want no witnesses to what we done

to Graham and the girl. In fact, Harris, there's no one alive that can testify for sure we were even at the place."

"What about Cole Randall? You said he was warned off."

Harris felt dazed, sickened. He heard himself asking questions of this man in front of him, his voice normal, his queries reasonable, and could hardly believe it was not all some ghastly joke Larn was playing on him.

"Hell," Larn said as he finished carefully tucking in his shirt, "Cole heard the warning shots. Then he bolted right back out through the gate. Didn't waste no time at all. I saw him coming back when he realized the ranchhouse was on fire. But it was dark. He couldn't have recognized any one of us from that distance. Riders, that's all he saw. We could just as well have been three saddle tramps that happened by."

"No," Harris said with emphasis, dismay stirring deep in his gut. "Cole will know." Still slumped in the wooden chair by Larn's desk, the banker shook his head wearily. "He'll know it was you. And he'll come looking for you—and me."

Larn shrugged into his coat and reached for a small brush he kept inside the trunk. "I suppose so. But no court could convict me or any of the boys on what Randall and the other riders with him saw."

"That's not the point! Cole Randall will be just like his father in this. He won't care what the law says. He won't wait for the law. And don't forget, I'm the one who killed his father."

Larn nodded, watching Harris carefully. "Guess that makes sense at that."

"You've got to stop him! You've still got your badges. You're still the law!"

"How much, Harris?"

"Damn you! I told you. Three thousand!"

"Stakes are higher now, banker. You're the target this time."

"And so are you!"

"I could ride out right now and leave you to handle Randall yourself."

"You wouldn't do that!"

"Sure, I would, Harris. I didn't kill Randall, so you don't owe me nothing. Best thing for me to do is cut my losses and ride for Texas."

Larn laughed openly when he saw the look of pure dismay on Harris's face.

"All right. All right, you son-of-a-bitch. All right. I'll pay."

"Damn right you will," Larn said, stepping close and slapping Harris across the face, hard.

The man's head swiveled under the force of the blow and tears of outrage crowded into his eyes.

"Next time you call me a son-of-a-bitch, banker," Larn said, "you better come armed." He stood back and regarded Harris speculatively. "I figure you might place a pretty high price on your life—say ten thousand?"

Harris considered the possibility of disputing this figure with Larn for only a moment. Then he nodded wearily, mopping his brow. Cold sweat stood out on it now as he realized what manner of men he was trapped between. There was little, indeed, to choose from.

"That's settled then. And I want five thousand for my men—for Miles and Gil Bonney."

Too beaten down by this time to argue, Harris just nodded wearily.

Larn was pleased. He studied Harris critically. "You look kind of green around the gills, Harris. You had your breakfast yet?"

"I'm not hungry."

"Well, I am. Think I'll mosey over to the hotel for breakfast. Join me if you want."

"Join *you?*"

"What's the matter? You too good for the man who does your killin' for you?"

Harris looked at Larn in something approaching despair. How could he count on this man—this cold-blooded animal—to stand between him and Cole Randall? Dully he remembered Larn saying something about other riders being with Cole when all this occurred. But he was too drained to pursue the matter.

He stood up wearily. "I'm going to the barber shop as soon as it opens. Then I'll be in my office."

"That's good, Harris. Because I think this time I'll want that money in advance."

"In advance? But . . ."

"You can trust me, Harris. I'm looking forward to stopping this guy Randall, myself. He's been pretty lucky up until now. Too damn lucky. But we'll be leaving soon as we can after the matter is settled. I figure it's best if we have the money already in our saddlebags."

"Yes . . . of course."

Harris walked wearily out into the street. He was so dazed that he turned right instead of left in heading for the barber shop. He caught himself and turned around. The morning sunlight was bright and warm, but that old premonitory chill had fallen over him again, this time so pervasive that it seemed to have seeped into the very marrow of his bones.

Ryan drove the Grahams' farm wagon. Nancy and Blue rode alongside, Cole riding point. The three bodies were wrapped in blankets in the wagon's bed. Two of the remains were barely recognizable as human, so badly charred were they. Cole's head bandage was grimy with the soot and parts of it were hanging loosely. Both his and Blue's faces and hands were blackened from poking among the charred beams and plaster, their boots and Levi's singed and burned in spots. Cole had insisted on recovering the bodies before the ruins of the ranchhouse had stopped smoldering.

The frame buildings that comprised Broken Bow looked

bright and newly washed in the early-morning sunshine. It was close to ten o'clock, Cole figured as he turned his mount down Main Street. He looked neither to the right nor to the left as he rode, not bothering to return the many startled looks that were sent his way from the townspeople who glanced up and saw the grim caravan. It wasn't until the wagon pulled up in front of Stitch Anderson's barber shop that a crowd gathered, materializing out of nowhere, it seemed to Cole, as he dismounted and strode through the crush and into the barber shop.

Stitch was on his way out. Cole told him who they had brought in—ignoring the wide-eyed citizen sitting in the barber chair with half his face lathered—and then told Stitch he would go upstairs for the doctor himself. He left the barber shop, fought his way through the crowd, then mounted the outside flight of steps to Doc Wilder's office.

He found the doctor hurriedly packing his black bag as a small town boy darted out through the door past Cole. Cole slumped into a chair and looked grimly at the doctor. Wilder hurried over to the door and closed it.

"My God, Cole," he said. "You look like the wrath of God."

"Maybe I am, Doc. I just finished poking through a piece of hell. That kid told you?"

"Three bodies, Tommy said."

"Linda Graham and Bill—and Cy Reese. Danny Larn burnt them out."

The doctor shook his head slowly, incredulously. "But why, Cole? *Why?* The Box W was no threat to Harris."

Cole explained the trap, the sequence of events when he rode into the Box W compound. When he finished, the doctor shook his head wearily.

"Madness," he muttered. "That's all it is. Madness."

The doctor's door opened and Eliot Trace ducked in. The lawyer looked distraught. "Cole, I just heard," he said. "It's a terrible thing. I know how you must feel."

"Do you, Trace?"

"Of course I do. But, Cole, you mustn't do anything foolish."

Cole's eyes narrowed. "Like what, Trace."

The man swallowed. "Harris and Danny Larn and his two remaining deputies are holed up in the bank—waiting for you."

"And how do you know that, Trace?"

"Harris talked to his lawyer this morning, and—"

Cole laughed shortly, derisively, cutting off Trace. "And Deal Wightman talked to you."

"Harris is frightened out of his mind, Cole. He thinks you're going to kill him."

"He should be and I am." Cole looked shrewdly at Trace. "He's frightened because he knows what happened at the Box W. Right, Trace?"

The lawyer nodded.

"Which means he knew about it long before the Doblers and I rode in. Now who do you suppose told him, Trace?"

"Yes . . . yes, of course, Cole, but—"

"Don't do anything foolish—that it, Trace?"

"Cole, the governor is sending one of his closest advisers here to investigate these killings. He'll arrive tomorrow and when he gets here Danny Larn will no longer be wearing a Deputy U.S. Marshal's badge."

"That's fine, Trace. But it doesn't change a thing."

"Damnit, Cole! How can you say that?"

"Tell me, Trace. Isn't Danny Larn still wearing a badge? And aren't those men riding with him still legally his deputies?"

Reluctantly, Trace nodded.

"Which means they can ride out anytime they want—legally. Hell, Trace, that murderer and his cutthroats are what passes for law in these parts—thanks to Maxwell Harris. And what about Harris? Can he be touched, *legally?*"

"Cole, you can't be judge, jury, and executioner in one. Then you *will* be in trouble with the law."

"Listen to me, Trace. I'm going to do what I should have done a long time ago—what Bill Graham told me I should do—what my father would have done in my place." He frowned and looked away from the lawyer momentarily. "My only regret is that I didn't listen to Bill then. If I had, maybe he—and Linda—would be alive now. And a lot of others besides."

Trace looked for a long moment at Cole, started to say something, then thought better of it. He turned and left the office.

The doctor stepped forward to unwind Cole's bandage, shaking his head as he did so. "I still say it's madness. All of it. Pure madness."

Cole said nothing and let the man's agile fingers undo the long bandage. His head was pounding, but all he wanted was for the doctor to inspect the wound and then give him a new bandage, one that was not hanging loosely about his neck and falling into his eyes when he most needed clear vision.

Twelve

DANNY LARN and Miles had been standing in the doorway to Danny's office when word of the grisly burden contained in Box W's wagon swept up Main Street. A towheaded kid was running along the boardwalk, telling the story to all who would listen. When he reached the U.S. Marshal's office, Danny detained him with a cruel, viselike grip on the biceps of the boy's right arm. He squeezed every scrap of information he could get out of the boy. Finished with him, he released the kid and moved swiftly out of the doorway and started along the boardwalk toward the bank, Miles keeping step with him.

"Harris will find out in a minute," he told Miles, a sardonic smile on his polished features, his eyes bright with anticipation. "He sure as hell will be ripe by the time we get there."

Miles stifled a cough and nodded, obviously as pleased as Danny.

"Get Gil," Danny said, "and the horses. Meet me at the bank."

Miles stepped off the boardwalk and hurried across the street to awaken Gil. Danny, in sight of the bank entrance now, saw a distracted Maxwell Harris emerge from the bank and look down the street toward him. The judge was with him. With a curt nod, Danny directed Harris back into the bank. Both men vanished inside.

There was a slight smile on Danny's face when he entered the bank a moment later. He pushed through the low gate and walked directly to Harris's office, ignoring the excited stares of the two clerks, and pushed open the door without knocking. Harris was standing at the window behind his desk, peering out. The judge was sitting back in the leather sofa along the wall under an impressive oil portrait of Harris. The judge had a full tumbler glass in his hand, a freshly opened bottle on the floor beside him.

He looked up as Danny entered and waved a hooked, rheumatic claw at him. "Behold! The Angel of Death appears!"

Danny ignored the judge and addressed Harris. "The party's starting a mite sooner than I expected. Cole Randall and the Doblers just brought in the bodies. Looks like they were the riders I saw with Randall. You got that money ready?"

Harris nodded and with his head indicated a large carpetbag on the floor in the corner. "It's in there."

"Good," said Danny, starting toward it.

Harris glanced nervously at the judge, then back at Danny. "It's . . . not all there, Larn."

Danny pulled up and turned to face the banker. "What are you trying to pull, Harris?"

The man moistened his full lips nervously. Before Danny's harsh stare he visibly faltered. "There's half of it in there. You get the other half when . . . the job is done."

"You mean when I kill Cole Randall."

"Yes . . . damn you! Yes!"

Danny swallowed the contempt he felt for this man—and the anger as well—and forced himself to smile. "All right, banker. But you better tell those clerks out there they got a holiday. Get rid of them."

Harris nodded, hurried out from behind his desk, and left the office. Danny looked at the judge, who had just about drained his glass. But he didn't look any the worse for it, and his eyes regarded Danny steadily.

"Drink, Danny Larn?" the judge asked, holding up the bottle. "Or don't you need anything with which to prop your courage."

"Guess not, lush."

"So I understand. The ascetic killer, Danny Larn. A true marvel, a god that makes rain, only the rain is not cats and dogs—but human corpses."

"You called me the Angel of Death," Danny said quietly. "Maybe I prefer that."

"Do you, now?"

"What did you mean—the ascetic killer?"

The judge poured whiskey into his glass, his grotesque hands shaking only slightly. "Ascetic," he said, "means you abstain from the normal pleasures of life. That is, you deny yourself material satisfaction—usually for religious reasons or convictions." He smiled at Danny. "Yes, I would say that fits you perfectly, Danny Larn. Your trade, your profession—your *religion*—is death, and you would have no distractions in your worship of that dark deity."

Danny was disturbed by the judge's words, and yet strangely elated at the same time. Was this what he was, after all? Did all this mean something then? And was this why he felt nothing—would *never* feel anything? Danny felt himself straighten up just a bit as he regarded the judge with a sudden tolerance.

"Aha!" said the man. "I see you approve. I have given you a purpose, have I?" He shook his head and drank heavily from the glass. "I have made you an instrument of a dark force—and you seize upon this with delight. So be it! Perhaps you have come for me as well." He looked closely at Larn. "Is that right, Danny Larn? Are you my deliverance too?"

Now the man's words made Danny uncomfortable. He had the feeling suddenly that this man was toying with him, using words to entrap him. Danny stepped back from the judge. "Shut up, Judge. Just drink your whiskey and shut up."

At that moment Harris reentered the office, his handkerchief in his hand as he mopped his now florid face. "They're gone," he told Danny. "I gave them the day off." He looked down at the judge. "You better get out of here too, Judge."

"No," Danny said, on sudden impulse. "He stays."

The judge saluted Danny with the bottle and poured himself another tumbler full of whiskey. Harris shrugged and moved past Danny to slump in his swivel chair behind the desk.

"What now, Larn?" the banker asked. "Word is Cole's gone to see Doc Wilder. Maybe he's still too badly hurt to come after us."

"If you believe that, you're a fool."

"Then what are you going to do? Just wait here for him to come to us?"

"Keep your britches on, banker, and let me handle this."

"It's your bungling that brought us to this pass!"

Danny simply nodded and walked to the window and looked out. Main Street appeared to be deserted as most of the storeowners and townspeople crowded about the barber shop. As Danny watched, he saw Miles and Gil coming with the horses. Both men were riding. As they reached the hitch rail in front of the bank, they dismounted.

Danny left the window and opened the office door to see Miles and Gil poking their heads into the bank.

"In here," Danny told them.

As soon as Miles and Gil joined him, Danny turned to Harris and lifted his Smith & Wesson from its holster. Aiming it almost negligently at the banker, he smiled and said, "Open up your safe in the other room and fill that carpetbag over there. You play games with me, banker, and I'll play them right back at you."

Harris paled. "But . . . that would be robbery!"

Danny laughed. Then he looked at Gil. "Get back to those horses and bring in all the saddlebags. And move!"

As Gil darted back out of the office, Danny turned his attention again to Harris and waggled his revolver impatiently. "Get a move on, banker, or I'll finish you for Cole Randall and take what's in that carpetbag!"

The man sprang hastily to his feet and brushed past Danny. Danny followed him to the safe, his revolver held inches from the man's head, as Harris got down on one knee and began to work the combination. He was coming apart at the seams, Danny noted, so he kept his own impatience under control as the banker fumbled at the dial. At last the tumblers clicked into place, Harris rose to his feet, and pulled open the massive door. Danny stepped back, and as soon as Harris was clear of the safe, he raised his revolver swiftly and brought its barrel down heavily onto the man's skull. The man dropped silently in his tracks.

"Get the carpetbag," Danny told Miles.

Gil had already brought in the saddlebags and Danny set him to work filling them. He went to the door of the bank then and looked out. The street was even more deserted than before. The crowd that had gathered about Box W's wagon was beginning to disperse. But there was no sign of Cole Randall or the Doblers.

Danny smiled thinly and hurried back to the safe. Miles was on one knee beside Gil, stuffing bills into the carpetbag.

"Hurry it up," Danny told them. "Looks like we won't have any trouble riding out. That fool, Randall, is nowhere in sight. I'm not afraid of the son-of-a-bitch, but he's lucky."

Miles began to cough violently. He ducked his head to ease the pull in his chest and hauled out his bandanna. After the spasm passed he glanced up at Danny through tear-wet eyes. "That's right, Danny. One thing we could never claim was we were lucky."

Danny nodded grimly down at Miles. "So hurry it up."

The office door opened wider suddenly and the judge appeared in the doorway, leaning precariously against the sill, a nearly empty bottle in one hand. "You disappoint me, Danny Larn," the old man said. "I thought you were of a larger, more impressive lineage—one of the four horsemen of the apocalypse, perhaps. Alas, you're just a garden-variety bank robber. How depressing."

Then the judge saw Harris's crumpled body. He hurried across the room and knelt by the banker's side. As soon as he discovered the deep laceration on Harris's skull, the man looked up at Danny in dismay.

"You might have killed him!"

"Hell, I thought I had."

By this time Gil and Miles had stuffed into the carpetbag and the saddlebags all the currency they could carry. The two men got to their feet and lugged the bags through the swing gate.

"That carpetbag goes on my saddle," Danny told Miles as he moved after them. He was holstering his revolver when he heard a soft scuttling sound just behind him.

He turned swiftly. The judge was bringing the whiskey bottle down on Danny's head. Before Danny could raise his arm to ward off the blow, the bottle caught him on the side of the head with such force it shattered, driving Danny to his knees. Danny did not lose consciousness. He fell back, away from the judge, drawing his revolver in a sudden, instinctive move.

The judge stood over Danny, swaying unsteadily, looking stupidly at the jagged neck of the bottle still clutched in his right hand. He blinked as if to clear his head. Then he focused on the muzzle of Danny's Smith & Wesson. Dropping the remains of the bottle, he straightened up as best he could, and waited.

"A momentary lapse, Danny Larn," the judge said musingly. "Too much alcohol. Everyone said it would be the death of me. So here I am, waiting for deliverance."

Larn understood, despite his spinning head. He felt no real anger toward the old fool as the blood trickled down the right side of his head. He fired twice carefully, pumping both slugs into the old man's chest. The judge bucked like a sheet in the wind, then collapsed to the floor. There was a faint smile on his face as he rolled over onto his back.

Danny shook his head to clear it as Miles, rushing back into the bank, bent over him.

"I'm all right," Danny said. "That crazy old buzzard broke that bottle of his over my head. Just let me rest here for a minute."

"Sure," said Miles, standing back.

Danny blinked and tried to stop the bank's floor from tipping under him. He held the floor with both hands and concentrated. At last the pounding in his head subsided to a steady ache. He looked up at Miles, still patiently watching him. A slight, reddish haze seemed to have filled the interior of the bank. Danny wondered how long he had been hanging onto the floor like this.

A shout came from the entrance. Gil was yelling something about Cole Randall and the Doblers. Danny cursed and held out his hand to Miles. Miles hauled him to his feet. Danny was steadying himself when he heard the sudden explosion of hoofs. Gil was taking off without them!

Thrusting savagely past Miles, Danny ran to the bank entrance and managed to send one round after the fleeing kid. The bullet went high, but it didn't matter. Two of the Doblers—armed with rifles—emerged from an alley as Gil swept toward them. Gil tried to cut them down with his six-gun, but he had always been a lousy shot. Both Doblers opened up and Gil peeled back off his horse.

"The son-of-a-bitch!" Danny muttered. "I was going to do that myself sooner or later."

Then Miles nudged Danny and pointed down the street in the other direction. Cole Randall and another Dobler were hurrying toward them.

Smiling grimly, Danny reached for the reins to his mount and swung into his saddle. "Come on, Miles. We'll make them turn tail or run the bastards down!"

"Suits me fine," said Miles, vaulting into his own saddle. The exertion caused him to start hacking and he fumbled momentarily with his reins. Danny waited patiently.

When Miles was ready, Larn bent low over his horse's neck and plunged his spurs deep into the animal's flanks. The powerful horse lunged forward, then pounded into a gallop, heading directly for the two men.

As Danny rode he felt the excitement building within him. Only at moments like this, he realized now, did he really feel alive. Angel of Death, was he? Well then, so be it. That was something, at least. . . .

Cole and Ryan pulled up in the middle of the street as Danny Larn and Miles Crocket galloped toward them. Larn and his deputies weren't interested in protecting Maxwell Harris, it seemed, after all—just in getting away with their bulging saddlebags. Harris had paid more for his protection than he had intended, Cole realized with some satisfaction. A swollen carpetbag attached to the side of Larn's saddle flopped wildly as Larn rode furiously closer.

"Don't move," said Cole, "until I give the word. Then

you duck to your left and I'll go right. Come up firing as they go by."

Ryan just nodded.

A second later Cole yelled, "Now!"

As Cole leaped to his right, he caught a glimpse of Larn's face leaning over his mount as he dug his spurs home. Cole struck the hard-packed dirt of the street awkwardly and rolled over once, then came up firing, levering his Winchester as rapidly as he could. Ryan too, resting on one knee, his six-gun held steady, was firing rapidly after the two men.

With a choking cry Miles took a round in his back. He threw up both hands and letting go of his reins toppled off his horse. For just a moment his boot caught in his stirrup. He slammed, shoulder first, onto the street's hard surface, was dragged a few yards, then dropped lifelessly in the dust as the horse continued to race away.

Cole cursed his throbbing head and tracked Larn, aware that if he missed this shot, the man might well get away. Abruptly, Larn reined in his mount. Whinnying in shrill distress at its handling, the horse almost foundered. Larn hauled the animal brutally around and raced back to the fallen Miles as Cole, astonished, lowered his rifle.

But Larn still had his six-gun out. Gleaming in the morning light, the Smith & Wesson jumped in Larn's hand as he swung from his saddle and fired at Cole.

Cole felt Larn's slug punch him in the right side, just below his ribs. It staggered him back, but he kept on his feet, tracked Larn as the man knelt beside Miles, and pumped a round into Larn's chest, high. Larn sagged, flung up his Smith & Wesson, and loosed another shot at Cole. But this one went high. Ryan caught Larn with a single bullet then, as Cole—his entire right side growing numb—squeezed off another shot. This time he knocked Larn forward over the consumptive's body.

His rifle still trained on Larn's prostrate form, Cole approached the man from one side, Ryan from the other. Larn was lying across his confederate's chest. Miles, it was obvious, was dead. Most likely he had been dead from the moment he struck the ground. His lifeless eyes stared up at Cole from out of their deep, haunted sockets. With the barrel of his rifle, Cole poked at Larn, then rolled him off Miles.

Larn was alive yet, the Smith & Wesson still in his right hand. He looked up at Cole and managed the ghost of a smile.

"Like Miles said," Larn managed, "we was never lucky. You're the lucky one. Not too bright, maybe. But lucky."

"That wasn't too bright," Cole said to Larn, "going back after a dead man."

"I know," Larn said, his voice faint, rasping. He frowned. "I don't understand."

Larn closed his eyes. The tremor that passed through his body was barely perceptible as the Smith & Wesson dropped from his lifeless fingers.

Cole turned then to face the bank. Ryan was standing beside him by this time and Nancy and Blue were running toward him. Cole started for the bank.

"'Where you going, Cole?" Ryan asked anxiously.

"Harris. It's not over yet . . . not while Harris lives. . . ."

Ryan let him go. Cole fell twice before he reached the bank entrance. As he started in, Nancy reached his side and began to plead with him. Cole shook his head violently without speaking, aware that he was losing blood rapidly. He couldn't let himself pass out now.

Nancy's face was close to his, pleading. Again he shook his head.

Blue pulled Nancy away as Cole lurched into the dim, cool interior of the bank. His eyes gradually adjusting to the dimness, he saw the still wide-open safe. The door to Harris's office was open, and as he started toward it, he stumbled over the shrunken body of Judge Warner. The man's bladder and his bowels had long since released in death and he stank powerfully.

The room spun sickeningly about Cole as he approached Harris's office. At last he caught sight of the man. He was sitting on the floor of his office, his back to his desk, the shotgun with which he had killed Cole's father in his hands. The entire left side of his face was caked with blood, and it appeared to Cole that the banker could see only out of his right eye.

Cole pulled up, and found himself staring into the shotgun's twin muzzles.

"Shoot, Harris, you son-of-a-bitch," Cole told the man, wondering at the same time why he found himself unable to bring his own rifle up.

The rifle was too heavy, Cole decided dully. He let it drop to the floor and drew his Colt. Still the banker did not fire on him. As Cole brought up his revolver and steadied it with his left hand, Harris let his shotgun slip to the floor.

"I can't kill you," the banker said, tipping his head slightly to see Cole more clearly. "But you can kill me easy enough. You should be proud, Cole. You are your father all over again. There isn't a trace of your mother in you. Go ahead. Shoot!"

Cole knew about his mother's thwarted love for this man and of his love for her. Always until this moment Cole had denied its significance. But he saw all at once how deeply it had cut—how this was the reason two men were now facing each other with murder in their hearts.

No more, Cole told himself with infinite weariness. *No more. End it here.*

Cole lowered his revolver.

"Shoot, damn you!" Harris croaked hoarsely. "You can't let me live—not after what I've done to you. You have to shoot me!"

Cole turned carefully and started from the bank, his right thigh heavy with his warm blood. As he emerged from the bank, the bright sunlight blinded him. He stumbled and felt himself falling. Hands caught him. He heard Nancy's voice. The brightness around him faded as he plunged into darkness.

Thirteen

NANCY REACHED the top of the bluff first. She pulled her mount to a halt and taking off her hat began to wave it. As Cole and Blue joined her, the train's engineer leaned on his whistle in a salute to Nancy. Ryan crested the ridge, took out his Colt, and pumped two shots into the late summer sky. From the bunting-draped train, winding like a bright toy through the valley below, there came a faint cheer.

Cole thought he could see Trace and Deal Wightman standing on the rear platform alongside all the dignitaries from Cheyenne, but he couldn't be sure. One thing was certain, however. Maxwell Harris had not ended his self-imposed exile in that hotel room of his for today's festivities. If he had, he would have been alone, not only on that rear platform, but on the train itself.

"Well, there she goes," Nancy said to Cole. "The Iron Horse has invaded the Circle C's valley. You don't seem too upset, Cole."

"It's a beautiful day, Nancy," he replied. "I've been cooped up for the best part of this summer, but I've still got the rest of August. There won't be any settlers swarming into this high country to slice up our grasslands, and five dollars an acre for all that government land is not such a bad price—not with the market price of beef going up the way it is." He grinned at her. "So why shouldn't I be pleased?"

"Cole Randall! Is that your order of priorities!"

"Why?" Cole asked, glancing at her brothers and winking. "Have I left anything out?"

"No," she said, suddenly clever, her eyes lighting maliciously. "Guess maybe you haven't left out a thing, at that."

She pulled her mount around and spurred the animal back down the slope, riding like an Indian, her long hair streaming out straight behind her.

Cole looked at Blue. "Suppose she's really riled?"

Blue shrugged. "Beats me, Cole. But I never did figure Nancy would stand for settling into a harness with any man—not the way she can ride and shoot."

Cole saw the gleam in both men's eyes. "Well, then. Guess I'll just have to ride after her and apologize."

"Better hurry it up," drawled Ryan. "She's near into the next county by now."

Cole spurred his horse down the slope after Nancy. As he felt the horse's powerful surge beneath him and the cool wind buffeting his face, he savored the awareness that he was nearly well again—in soul as well as in body. He had not killed Harris because he was not his father in all ways—only in those that he himself chose. And he chose not to play God. He chose not to rule over this valley like some

Old Testament Jehovah. Harris had been wrong. There was a trace of his mother in him—perhaps more than a trace. . . .

Cole saw he was gaining on Nancy. She looked back over her shoulder, laughed, tugged her hat down more firmly, then let out her mount. With a cry Cole dug his spurs into his horse and again closed the gap between them. As he swept through the valley's sweet, high grasses, he realized that he would be content to ride like this forever.

Only he knew that soon now Nancy would pull up. She always did. And that would be all right, too.

The Biggest, Boldest, Fastest-Selling Titles in Western Adventure!

★★★★★★★★★★★★★★★★★★
CHARTER'S MOST WANTED LIST

Merle Constiner

_81721-1 TOP GUN FROM THE DAKOTAS $2.50

_24927-2 THE FOURTH GUNMAN $2.50

Giles A. Lutz

_34286-8 THE HONYOCKER $2.50

_88852-6 THE WILD QUARRY $2.50

Will C. Knott

_29758-7 THE GOLDEN MOUNTAIN $2.25

_71146-4 RED SKIES OVER WYOMING $2.25

Benjamin Capps

_74920-8 SAM CHANCE $2.50

_82139-1 THE TRAIL TO OGALLALA $2.50

_88549-7 THE WHITE MAN'S ROAD $2.50

Raw, fast-action adventure from one of the world's favorite western authors

MAX BRAND
writing as Evan Evans

0-515-08571-5	MONTANA RIDES	$2.50
0-515-08527-8	OUTLAW'S CODE	$2.50
0-515-08528-6	THE REVENGE OF BROKEN ARROW	$2.75
0-515-08529-4	SAWDUST AND SIXGUNS	$2.50
0-515-08582-0	STRANGE COURAGE	$2.50
0-515-08611-8	MONTANA RIDES AGAIN	$2.50
0-515-08692-4	THE BORDER BANDIT	$2.50

*Blazing heroic adventures
of the gunfighters of the WILD WEST
by Spur Award-winning author*

LEWIS B. PATTEN

____ **GIANT ON HORSEBACK**	0-441-28816-2/$2.50
____ **THE GUN OF JESSE HAND**	0-441-30797-3/$2.50
____ **THE RUTHLESS RANGE**	0-441-74181-9/$2.50
____ **THE STAR AND THE GUN**	0-441-77955-7/$2.50